OVER BYRON BAY

OVER BYRON BAY

JANE ELLYSON

OVERBYRONBAY.COM

A catalogue record for this book is available from the National Library of Australia.

ISBN: 978-0-6481892-3-7

Editor: Jackie Bates

Internal formatting by Lisa Hannan Fox

Cover Design by c8v_logos on Fiverr

Photo on cover taken at McLeods Shoot, N.S.W. by author

www.overbyronbay.com

Praise for Over Byron Bay

Poor timing and agonies of conscience are ever present in this sweet love story.

Jackie Bates

Jane takes us away to her special part of the world in this touching tale of the past and the present coming together. Will love be refound?

Carlotta Mendelson

An enjoyable holiday read where love conquers all.

Diane Michelle

CONTENTS

FAMILY TREES

THE BOURNES & BRINKLEYS

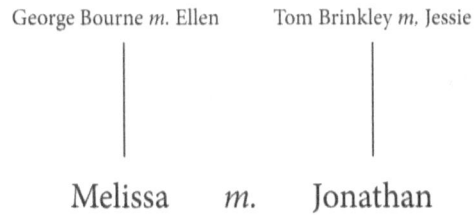

George Bourne *m.* Ellen   Tom Brinkley *m,* Jessie

Melissa   *m.*   Jonathan

THE WYATTS

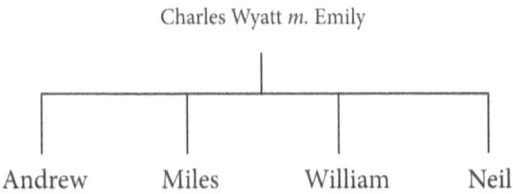

Charles Wyatt *m.* Emily

Andrew   Miles   William   Neil

MAP

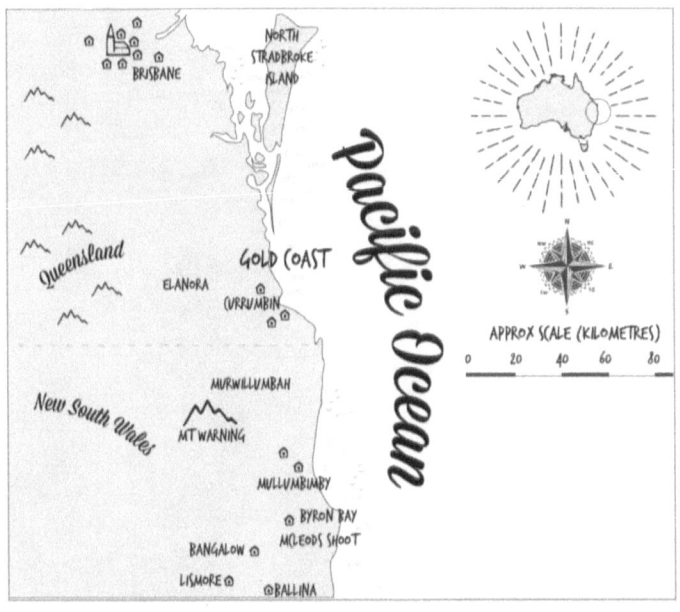

OCTOBER

*M*elissa Brinkley walked cautiously through the foyer of the small church and sat in the last pew. Emily Wyatt's sudden death had deeply shocked and disturbed her. Emily, along with her husband Charles and their sons, had been neighbours of her parents for many years, and she was grateful that a fleeting visit home allowed her to attend the funeral. The sweet scent of frangipanis filled the small church and she smiled as she remembered that these striking yellow and white flowers had been her friend's favourite.

The congregation stood as the funeral party entered the church. Melissa was relieved that Andrew Wyatt didn't seem to have noticed her presence at his mother's funeral. Andrew followed his brothers to the front pew, twirling a single frangipani blossom between his fingers. Watching him from the back of the church, she didn't think he'd changed much in the last five years. His curly hair had been cropped, and he'd lost a little weight which made his muscular features more prominent. He's still handsome, she thought. After what had happened at graduation, she'd been confused about her feelings. She'd never spoken to him about it, but he was one of the reasons she'd taken the job at Alcock Architects in Boston. She'd wanted to put as many miles between them as possible, hoping time and distance would change how she felt.

Her thoughts were interrupted by the playing of *Amazing Grace*. The congregation stood to sing the familiar hymn and then sat down awkwardly to listen to a eulogy read by a family friend. The dulcet tones of the church's organ this time indicated the end of the service. The congregation rose as Emily's coffin was carried out by her four sons, Andrew, Miles, William and Neil, heads bowed as they carried the casket out of the church. She waited several minutes until the church had emptied before gathering up her handbag and scarf, and walked towards the doors. She was surprised to discover Andrew waiting for her in the foyer. For a brief moment they stood and looked intently into each other's eyes, unsure of what to say.

'Thank you for coming,' he said softly. His opening words served to ease the tension between them. 'Mum would be pleased you're here.'

Melissa nodded.

'I'm sorry about your Mum's passing.'

'Thank you,' he replied, pausing for a moment. 'How long are you home for?'

'Three weeks,' she said. 'I have some personal stuff to sort out.'

Andrew nodded, and paused before continuing, 'You look lovely.'

'She certainly does,' interrupted Miles Wyatt, who strode into the foyer looking for his brother. 'Hello Melissa – good to see you.'

'Nice to see you too,' she said, 'although I would have preferred different circumstances.' Miles nodded and put his hand on Andrew's shoulder.

'Andrew, the car's ready. Time to go.'

He turned to Melissa, leaned forward and brushed his lips against her cheek. His lips were soft and the distinctive scent of cinnamon aftershave brought all the memories and feelings from their university days flooding back. Nothing had changed. Trembling, she closed her eyes. When she opened them he was still there, watching her. He turned and walked quickly down the steps leading from the church.

NOVEMBER – PART 1

The three weeks since Melissa arrived home had flown by. Her father ensured she had little time on her own, arranging many reunions with her friends and family. She'd promised Jonathan she'd be home by Thanksgiving, which was by now only three days away. He'd rung only once since she'd arrived to see how things were going. She was grateful for this as she needed space to sort out her feelings.

She'd met Jonathan within the first week of arriving in Boston five years ago. Her emotions had been in turmoil, and his friendship had quickly helped to dull the pain. Jonathan was good looking and easy going. His tanned skin and crinkly eyes were the result of many hours spent outdoors. Two years later, they were married. The wedding was a small one, just Jonathan's parents and her father – Melissa's mother, Ellen, had been dead for nearly ten years. Married life initially had been great, but lately, Jonathan's job as a surveyor had involved frequent travel, and he was often away for several weeks at a time. Whenever they were together, they seemed to spend an increasing amount of time arguing. When Jonathan announced that he had to work in a remote area of Alberta, Canada for six weeks, she decided to take time out from work to come home and make sense of her unhappiness.

Home, she had mused, it feels a million miles away.

'Home' was Bangalow, a small town in northern New South Wales, sixty-five kilometres south of the state border with Queensland. Bangalow had always been in her heart her home, although she had been born of an American mother. Her parents had met at an agricultural conference in Maine. It was the only time her father had ventured outside of Australia and his friends were amused that he not only loved the experience but had come home with a foreign fiancée. Her father now lived alone in a lovingly restored Federation-style house, with high ceilings and decorative gables. He'd stopped teaching science at the Southern Cross University in nearby Lismore when Ellen had died and now ran cattle and harvested fruit on their land. Their nearest neighbours were the Wyatts, who lived a short distance away on the other side of Byron Creek. The Wyatt family had lived beside the Bourne family for twenty years, although Melissa's friendship with Emily Wyatt only developed

5

shortly before her mother's death and continued by correspondence, after she left for the States. Emily had been her comforter and her friend. She'd shared everything with Emily except for her feelings of confusion over her friendship with Andrew. Melissa had planned to change this on her visit home, but fate had intervened. Suddenly she felt very alone.

On Tuesday morning, Melissa checked in online and booked one night's accommodation at the Brisbane Hilton. Her father had tried to persuade her to let him drive her to the airport early Wednesday morning, but it was a two-hour car journey from Bangalow to Brisbane airport and she knew he was no longer confident driving beyond the local area. He had become a very old sixty-five-year-old.

'Besides,' she explained, 'I want to get in some last-minute shopping in the mall.' She hugged her father and kissed him goodbye. 'I promise that I won't leave it so long between visits in the future.' George Bourne nodded. There was a glint in his eye, which Melissa knew was a tear. She drove away quickly, knowing he'd be embarrassed if she saw him cry. He'd aged so much since her mother died – she suspected he was willing himself to die too. She made a mental note to call him every day.

It was a beautiful, clear, azure blue day as she turned left on to the Hinterland Way and headed north for Brisbane. She felt an overwhelming sense of sadness as she left the last traces of settlement and headed out through the rolling hills behind Byron Bay. At McLeods Shoot, Melissa pulled the car on to the verge to take in the sweeping view from Mount Warning to Byron Bay Light-house. Dolphins were riding the mile-long waves in the distance and eagles soared high above the hills. She sighed as she pulled the car out on to the Pacific Highway again and settled in for the drive north.

She checked into her hotel room and quickly show-ered, looking forward to an afternoon of shopping in Queen Street Mall. The phone in her room was ringing as she stepped out of the bathroom.

'Melissa, it's Andrew.'

She sat down on the bed and caught her breath.

'I was hoping to catch you before you left. Your dad told me where you were staying. I was wondering if we could meet somewhere – today. I need to talk to you – well to give you something, actually.'

'Oh,' was all she could say.

'My mother left you something and I was hoping to give it to you before you flew out.'

'Where would you like to meet?' Melissa said calmly, having regained her composure.

'How about Il Centro by the river?'

'Lovely,' she smiled into the phone. 'I'll see you at one.'

'Great. I look forward to it.'

Melissa returned the phone to its cradle but remained seated on the bed for several moments.

What would Emily want to give me?' she wondered. She opened her suitcase to examine the contents and quickly decided upon a white and gold linen suit and a pair of pearl earrings. Melissa knew she looked confident although the impression was only an illusion, disguising the tumultuous way she felt.

Andrew was already seated when she arrived at the restaurant. He stood as she approached the table, reached out for both her hands, and brought her close towards him.

'I'm so pleased I was able to get hold of you before you flew out – we've so much to catch up on.'

She said nothing, but nodded in agreement, as she sat down in the chair being offered by the waiter.

'So,' he continued, 'did you manage to resolve everything?'

'You never were a shrinking violet, were you Andrew Wyatt?'

'Well, we used to be able to share anything with each other,' Andrew returned.

'That was a long time ago.'

'It wasn't that long ago – and some things never change.'

'Maybe,' she paused. 'Why don't you tell me what you've been doing these last five years?'

'That's a pretty good diversionary question which I'll let you get away with just this once,' he smiled. 'I always pictured myself as the high flying corporate lawyer - working for a prestigious firm, bringing in the big dollars, driving a convertible BMW – well, that's what I've got - but it doesn't feel as good as I imagined it would. Some of my clients have values I just don't identify with – and I don't feel like I'm doing anything worthwhile, or that gives something back.' He paused and looked into the bottom of his wine glass. 'So, I've accepted a position with the Queensland Legal Aid Commission, starting in a month's time.'

'And it only took you five years to figure it out,' she teased him. 'Not bad, Wyatt.'

'Of course, I would have figured it out a lot sooner if you'd been here to set me straight,' he retorted, laughing.

'Ah, but sometimes we need to struggle with the pain of a poor decision to learn what should have been obvious from the start.'

He looked deeply into her eyes.

'I've missed you. Why did you go away?'

'I guess I needed to make a poor decision,' she replied matter-of-factly.

'The menu, madam and sir,' the waiter interrupted.

His timing didn't suit Andrew, but provided Melissa with the opportunity to avoid answering his searching questions.

'The soup of the day is pumpkin and smokehouse

bacon swirled with cream, and the Chef's recommendation for the main meal is baked barramundi.'

They perused the menu, but both were distracted by the direction in which their conversation was heading.

'The special sounds lovely,' said Melissa.

'Make that two Chef's specials,' Andrew added, anxious to get rid of him.

He looked at Melissa, and raised his glass to hers. She smiled and lifted her wine glass to his. 'Here's to,' he paused, 'fewer poor decisions.'

'Agreed,' she responded as their glasses clinked.

'Oh,' he said as he remembered the reason for their lunch. He reached into his pocket, pulled out a small velvet covered box and placed it on the table in front of her. 'Mum's gift to you.'

She opened the box. Inside was a beautiful antique bracelet, set alternately with emeralds and rubies. She stared at the bracelet, overwhelmed by its beauty.

'Well try it on, silly,' he said, breaking her trance. He removed the bracelet from its case and fastened the clip around her wrist.

'Beautiful,' she said softly. She looked up from the bracelet to find Andrew watching her intently. She smiled at him and then quickly returned to examining the bracelet.

The waiter brought their meals, which they hardly touched as they enjoyed sharing stories. Their conversation was filled with warmth and laughter, but avoided moving to difficult areas. A sharp signal from Andrew's phone abruptly interrupted their conversation. He grimaced as he read the message. He looked at his watch and smiled. 'Oops – did you realise it's half past three? Unfortunately, very unfortunately I have to get back to the office. I'm s'posed to be in a meeting.'

She nodded and stood up to say goodbye. He took her left hand and brought her closer to him. He leaned forward and kissed her gently on the lips. His lips were soft and warm. Her heart started beating quickly.

'It's been so good to see you' he said. He ran his finger down the side of her face. His phone again started beeping, furiously demanding his attention.

They said their goodbyes and Andrew picked up his briefcase, thrust three hundred-dollar bills into the surprised waiter's hand and strode out of the restaurant, and out of her life once more. She sat down, picking up her half-empty glass of white wine and started swirling the contents around absentmindedly. She took a sip, and smiled as she remembered the warmth of the afternoon's discussion. Her eyes took in the gentle activity on the Brisbane River. The paddle steamer, the *Kookaburra Queen,* moved gracefully up the river until it had passed under the Story Bridge and out of sight. This time tomorrow, she'd be on a plane en route to Boston. She'd given Boston and Jonathan so little thought since she'd been away. He'd be back from Canada within the week and she knew she'd have to have made a decision about the future by then.

She picked up her handbag and made her way back to the hotel. All the shops were closing as she strolled up Edward Street and she smiled as she reflected on how different her 'shopping' afternoon had been to what she'd expected.

NOVEMBER – PART 2

*B*ack at the hotel, she relaxed in the bath for over an hour and took time brushing her dark, shoulder-length hair. Her thoughts returned to their graduation dinner, five years previously. It had initially been a magical evening. She'd moved easily among Andrew's friends.

Friends, good friends – that was all she'd ever been, or ever wanted from Andrew, until that evening. The situation had suited them both. Melissa had relished the freedom of living away from her parents while she was at Uni. A serious relationship would have been a threat to her new life. Andrew's attitude was very similar, although in contrast to Melissa, who avoided being involved with anyone, Andrew had had a string of relationships – never long or serious. They never discussed them, and they'd never been a threat to their friendship.

She'd been enjoying her third glass of wine that evening when Angela Morton joined her. Angela was in her second year in business studies and was Andrew's current girlfriend. She had short dark curly hair and beautiful olive skin. 'It's been a lovely evening, hasn't it?' Angela offered.

Melissa nodded and smiled. 'Only twelve months until it's your turn,' she said.

'Well, twenty-four months actually – I'm going to defer Uni for twelve months so I can travel to Europe with Andrew next year.'

'Oh,' was all Melissa could reply. She was stunned. Although they'd never formalised their plans, they'd often talked about spending six months travelling through Europe by rail. Melissa was overcome with jealousy and betrayal. She hurried out of the ballroom, heading nowhere in particular, but anxious to put distance between herself and Angela. She'd regained her composure by the time she reached the edge of the car park.

'You're being ridiculous,' she scolded herself, 'what are you getting upset about, anyway? It's not that big a deal.' She managed to calm herself and sat on a low wall to try to make sense of her feelings. She didn't understand the pit in the bottom of her stomach. It was slowly dawning on her that she cared far more deeply for Andrew than she'd ever admitted to herself. She sighed, stood up, and ran her fingers through her hair. Her pride made her determined to hide her feelings from him. She returned to the ballroom.

Andrew and Angela were sitting with friends. Melissa forced a smile as she approached the table. He looked up at her quizzically.

'May I have the pleasure of your company for the next dance?' she asked politely.

'Certainly,' he returned with a wide smile. She could see Angela was not impressed. They moved easily around the dance floor together. 'Where have you been?' he whispered softly in her ear, 'I've missed you.' Melissa was furious, but maintained her composure.

'I've been around – talking to Graeme, and Angela, actually Angela was telling me about your planned overseas trip together.'

'Ahh,' he closed his eyes and grimaced.

'Look Andrew, I know that our trip was only a vague idea, maybe just a fool's dream – but I would have appreciated you telling me the dream had ended, rather than hearing it through Angela.'

'It's a little bit complicated,' he replied sheepishly.

'I'm sure it is,' she retorted sarcastically. He hadn't denied what Angela had said. It was obviously true. The song ended and the dancers reluctantly returned to their seats. Melissa was grateful for the opportunity to end their dance and conversation. She was feeling hurt and far less in control of her emotions than she'd planned in the car park. He seemed momentarily lost for words.

'Thank you for the dance,' he said at last.

She nodded, turned and left the ballroom. As she approached the outside steps, she heard footsteps behind her.

'Melissa,' he called out. She stopped but didn't turn around. 'We need to talk,' he continued.

'What else is there to say?' she replied without turning around.

'Stop being so bloody-minded'.

'Go to hell,' she returned. The tears had begun to stream down her face. She was determined not to let him see her this way. She ran to her car, and drove to her friend Lisa's place to stay the night. The following week she was on her way to Boston. She'd received an interesting offer of work that she'd previously been undecided about. Not anymore. She was going. And as far away from Andrew Wyatt as possible.

Two gentle knocks on the door interrupted her thoughts and dragged attention from the pain of that evening to the reality of her marbled bathroom. She tightened the sash on her midnight-blue, satin dressing gown and walked to the door. She was startled to see Andrew standing in the hallway.

'You forgot the bracelet's case, or I must have

collected it accidentally,' he said sheepishly as he passed the case to her.

'Thank you,' she said. She hesitated for a moment. Should she ask him in? Was that foolish? Maybe they did need to talk. 'Would you like a coffee?'

He nodded and walked past as she held the door open. As she filled the kettle, and found the coffee cups, she was aware that he was watching her. He was leaning on the archway to the kitchenette with a thoughtful expression on his face. Neither spoke as she poured the water and added the milk. She'd made hundreds of cups of coffee for him so didn't think to ask him how he liked it. As she passed him his cup, he said softly, 'Where did we go wrong?'

She put her coffee cup down to avoid scalding herself and looked directly at him.

'It's too late.' She dropped her head and looked at her bare feet, unable to meet his eyes any longer.

'I'm not going to let you run away from this conversation. It's been too long coming.' He stepped closer towards her. 'Please look at me.'

As she looked up, she was aware of how close he was standing to her. Her heart started beating rapidly. She opened her mouth to speak, but Andrew covered her mouth with his, and kissed her long and deeply. She didn't want him to stop. His hands slipped beneath her dressing gown and held her gently. Her gown floated to the floor and rested at her feet. Waves of passion surged through her body. Suddenly he released her.

'I'm sorry – you look so lovely – I feel so ...'

'Shhh,' she whispered. 'Don't say anything.'

For a few moments, they both stood silently, gazing into each other's eyes. Melissa shifted the weight between her feet and felt her nightdress strap fall from her shoulder. Andrew reached up to return the strap to her shoulder but stroked the side of her arm instead. Neither spoke. He ran his finger down her graceful neck and along the top of her nightdress. She closed her eyes momentarily and sighed. When she opened her eyes, Andrew was watching her closely. He slipped his hand under her nightie and cupped her breast with his hand. Her nipples hardened at his touch and he stroked them gently with his thumb. Melissa had never felt so naked, so sensual, and so wanting to make love. She pushed her left strap off her shoulder and her nightdress joined her dressing gown on the floor in a crumpled heap. Andrew's eyes devoured her.

'My God, you're beautiful,' he sighed.

In one swift movement, he swept her up in his arms and carried her into the bedroom.

'Melissa,' he said gently, 'I want to...'

She smiled and started unbuttoning his shirt. She slipped her hands under his shirt and stroked his chest. He undressed quickly and lay down on the bed beside her. He had waited so long for this moment that he was determined to savour every minute. He pulled her towards him and kissed her again. As his tongue probed deeper and deeper within her mouth, she could feel a pulsating rhythm between her legs. His lips followed the line of her neck until he once again found her breasts. He nuzzled each nipple between his teeth and gently removed her lace underwear.

His hand moved over her breasts, along her stomach and down to her pubic mound. He stroked her dark curly tufts gently and began to expertly explore the warm, moist folds between her legs. Melissa groaned. She could feel his firm, smooth penis rocking against her leg. She rolled on her side and guided his penis towards the gentle throbbing. He entered her slowly, determined to relish every moment. She arched her back, and grasped his penis with her inner muscles. He rolled on top of her and surged forward. All thought of control was lost as he responded to her urging for him. Melissa clenched her teeth and sighed as tiny explosions erupted in her body. Andrew shivered as he came, moments later.

Neither felt the need to speak, as they lay together in each other arms their eyes and hands were communicating perfectly.

'Well,' said Melissa after several minutes, 'should I warm up the coffee?'

He smiled at her. 'I'd rather warm you up again'. His lips moved to her breasts and down to her navel. She gasped as he began to explore between her legs with his tongue. She had never known love in this way and was overwhelmed by the sensations sweeping over her. As she raced quickly towards another orgasm, he stopped kissing her and entered her. They both cried out with joy as they climaxed together. They made love once again an hour later, and then fell asleep, sated, in each other's arms.

The chiming of Brisbane's Town Hall clock woke Melissa from a deep sleep. She rolled over to kiss Andrew and was surprised to find him gone. There was a note on his pillow.

Dear Melissa,

Last night was wonderful. You looked so beautiful this morning that I couldn't bear to wake you. Please call me at work before you go on 073 2 29 96 88 – we need to talk. I love you. Andrew

She shut her eyes and smiled. Last night hadn't been a dream. She picked up his pillow and hugged it. The fragrance of his cinnamon aftershave still lingered and she drank it in as she reflected on their night of lovemaking.

The phone beside the bed rang. She picked it up excitedly, expecting to hear his voice. Instead she heard nothing but static.

'Hello? Hello there?' she repeated.

'Melissa, is that you? It's Hank Matthews.'

Hank was one of Jonathan's colleagues and close friends.

'Yes Hank?' she said, cautiously.

'Um, I'm afraid I have some bad news – there's been an accident ...'

She knew Jonathan was dead before Hank told her.

She ran the details of the accident over again in her mind. He had been driving back to his apartment, late at night, when his front tyre had blown out. The car had swerved across the road, smashed into a tree and exploded within seconds. There were two bodies in the car, the second yet to be identified. It didn't feel real. Melissa was in a daze. She mechanically packed her bags, and caught a taxi to the airport. Her trance was broken momentarily by an announcement on the airport's public-address system. She went to the information desk and collected a telephone message from Andrew.

'Please call me before you leave,' it said simply.

She longed to talk to him, but couldn't bring herself to make the call. At the time of the accident she'd been in bed with him. She doubted she could ever forgive herself. She was grateful that the seat beside her in the plane was unoccupied, as she didn't feel capable of talking to anyone. Jonathan's parents were waiting for her as she emerged from Customs. In an instant, Jonathan's death became a reality. She sobbed uncontrollably in her mother-in-law's arms from feelings of grief, guilt and physical exhaustion. They took her home with them, and she stayed at their house for the next two weeks, until the day of the funeral. The nature of the accident had necessitated an enquiry, which had delayed the time until they could bury him. On her behalf, Mr and Mrs Brinkley refused all visitors and callers. They recognised that she needed to rest and to think about the future.

Melissa had regained her composure, but didn't feel well, on the day of the funeral. She was overwhelmed by the number of people she didn't know. These people were Jonathan's friends, but she didn't know them. This surely showed how far they'd grown apart. This made her feel even worse as she attempted to thank each person, for his or her support.

Jonathan's parents dropped her home at dusk after the funeral. She was pleased to be on her own, although the apartment looked eerie and felt lifeless. The lack of air over the last five weeks had made each room smell dank and dusty. She quickly opened windows to return a sense of life. As the evening light flooded into every corner of the room, Melissa looked around in amazement. She'd always thought the apartment was modern and sleek, decked out with black leather, modern sculptures and steel. But now she saw her home through different eyes. The interior of the apartment was black and shiny, and the evening shadows from the pine trees outside swayed slowly on the dining room walls. The apartment felt cold, lifeless and without heart – like a gallery where you never quite feel at ease, instead of a haven where you can put your feet up and feel secure. She now knew why Jonathan's parents had never seemed to want to spend time here; they simply hadn't felt comfortable.

Five weeks' worth of mail sat in a pile on the floor. There were bills to be paid, and letters of condolence from friends and colleagues to be read. Her father's handwriting was reassuringly familiar. She opened the envelope.

Darling Melissa,

How dearly I miss you and wish that you were still here with me.

I can imagine that the last weeks have been very difficult for you – trying to respond to people's kind wishes while dealing with your own grief.

I can easily recall my own sense of loss at your mother's death – and the lingering pain. Time helps of course but sometimes I hear a song or I smell an iceberg rose and she is here with me. And then I remember that she isn't, and loneliness is all I feel. I miss her, I miss her so much, and I miss you.

Will you come home? I can look after you. I don't want you to be alone.

Dad

She wiped a tear from her eye, and put the letter back in its envelope. It was still too soon to make decisions. She needed to sort out Jonathan's belongings and put order back into her life. But that could wait until tomorrow. She was exhausted so shuffled into their bedroom and lay down without taking off her clothes. Within moments a deep sleep embraced her.

EARLY DECEMBER

*M*elissa was roused by the sound of rush hour traffic and it momentarily confused her. She opened her eyes and scanned the room. The reality of where she was and why she was here, alone, came quickly back to her. She showered, dressed and prepared toast and tea for breakfast. A nagging feeling of nausea remained, so she drank her tea and deposited the toast in the kitchen tidy.

The telephone rang as she was packing the dishwasher. Jonathan's solicitors were calling to arrange a time when they could discuss probate.

'This afternoon will be fine,' she heard herself reply.

She moved into the bedroom and began systematically opening drawers and wardrobes. In just over an hour she had gathered all of Jonathan's clothes and possessions into three sacks. It struck her as strange that three small sacks represented all that was left over from a full life. As she stood and reflected, she noticed Jonathan's travel luggage standing by the bedroom door.

This must have been the case that Jonathan had with him in Canada, she thought.

She guessed that one of Jonathan's colleagues had dropped it off last week when she was still staying with his parents. It was too heavy to lift so she dragged it across the lounge room and propped it open against the divan. Inside the case, in neat and ordered piles, were Jonathan's jumpers, shirts, underclothes and books. As she removed the books from the case, several photos fell to the floor. There were two photos, one of the Canadian Rockies, and one of Jonathan with his arm slung casually over the shoulder of a woman Melissa didn't recognise. Jonathan and the woman were both laughing. Melissa stared at the photo of the smiling woman with the fair skin, hair cropped short at the back and with a long fringe. While she didn't recognise her, there was some-thing familiar. There was something about the eyes. Melissa had seen those eyes before. Was she one of the people Melissa had met at the funeral?'

A gentle knock at the door interrupted her thoughts. Melissa looked at her watch and guessed that it was Jonathan's mother with a chicken casserole. She knew that Jessie and Tom had been worrying about her not eating. She opened the door and gasped. Standing on the porch, looking unshaven and weary, was Andrew. He must have just flown in, and looked like he'd had little sleep on the flight. She smiled at him but said nothing as she opened the door wider to invite him in. He walked into the living room and surveyed the surroundings. He kept his back turned as he said, 'When you didn't call I was so worried. I waited twenty-four hours, but I couldn't stand it, so I rang your dad. He gave me your mobile number and told me what happened. Then I understood.'

He turned to face her, but she brushed past him and walked quickly into the kitchen, blinking back the tears.

'I'm so sorry. I wanted to call you straight away but I knew that what I had to say, you had to hear directly from me.'

He followed her into the kitchen and stood behind her.

'I don't want to lose you again. I couldn't stand it. I was a fool to deny what I felt for you. I want to be with you always. I want to see your smile last thing at night and to wake up each day and see your face on the pillow beside mine.'

Melissa didn't hear this last word as she had fainted into his arms.

The feeling of starched sheets and the sharp smell of antiseptic were the first indications that Melissa was somewhere unfamiliar. She opened her eyes and surveyed the room. White walls and grey linoleum said more about the hospital's need for dull consistency than style. She heard footsteps approaching so looked towards the open doorway.

'You've not been eating very well, I hear.'

An elderly gentleman in a white coat, with horn rimmed spectacles stood smiling in the doorway.

'Has my mother-in-law been telling stories?' Melissa smiled as she replied.

'Whilst I have a duty to protect my sources, I think that I could safely say that the very tired looking young man in the corridor is not your mother-in-law. Your husband perhaps?'

Melissa shook her head gently, and looked up as Andrew walked in.

'I see that you have company, so I'll pop back in to see you when I have completed my rounds.'

The doctor nodded to Andrew as he walked out the door. He pulled up a chair close to her bed and rested his hand on top of hers. His tired eyes looked into hers and he smiled.

'You know, it's very obvious to me that someone needs to look after you.'

'Yes?' she replied, holding back her own smile.

'We can't have you dropping to the floor wherever you are with no one to pick you up.'

'Really, I'm fine.' She looked deeply into his eyes and

continued. 'I've just been too tired to sleep, to eat or to make decisions. But now, I'm beginning to see things a little more clearly.' Melissa paused, and Andrew stopped smiling and closed his eyes, as if afraid of what he was about to hear. 'I need to start my life all over. And I need to do it alone. I have to put the past behind me and move forward. I feel so confused, and so guilty.'

'And what do you feel for me?' he asked.

She paused again and closed her eyes.

'I can't ever remember feeling so secure, and so loved as when I was with you that night. But every time I remember that evening, I remember the pain and the guilt that followed. And it is destroying me, and will slowly destroy us if we stay together. And I couldn't stand that.'

He rested his head in both hands and said nothing.

At last he asked, 'Is that what you really want?'

She looked at him intensely and then out of the hospital window.

'Yes,' was all she could whisper in reply.

He left the room as she broke down and wept.

'Is everything OK?'

Melissa opened her eyes and found the kindly doctor watching her with deep concern. She nodded and smiled as he pulled up a chair close to the bed.

'So how are you feeling now?' he asked gently.

'I'm still a little tired' she replied.

'Well, that's to be expected for a woman in your situation.'

Melissa was surprised by his directness and wondered who had told him about Jonathan's death. She certainly hadn't, and she doubted whether Andrew would have made any comment. She looked quizzically at the doctor who sensed that something was amiss so continued talking.

'Loss of appetite, tiredness, and feelings of nausea are common ailments in the first few months of pregnancy, so there's no need to be concerned. What is important is that you pay even more attention to eating properly, getting some regular gentle exercise and plenty of sleep.'

The doctor looked at her expecting a reply.

She was stunned, unable to respond. There was no doubt that it was Andrew's child as she'd not been intimate with Jonathan in months.

'That's all pretty straight forward, isn't it?' he asked.

Melissa simply nodded.

'Good,' the doctor said. 'Would you like to come back and see me in a month for a check-up?'

She looked at him, and then out of the window.

'Thank you, Doctor, but no,' she replied at last. 'I'm going home to Australia, so I'll visit my own doctor there.'

'Lucky you,' the doctor returned with a smile. He

stood to leave. 'You're well enough to go when you're ready.'

'Thank you, Doctor. Thank you for everything.'

'My pleasure,' he replied as he left the room.

Melissa drew circles on her midriff with the tips of her fingers trying to feel the baby growing inside and smiled. I'm going to have a baby, she reflected.

And then she remembered she'd just sent the baby's father away. Her moment of happiness was shattered.

She called in to see Jonathan's parents on her way home from hospital. She had some big news to share with them and knew they'd probably been wondering where she was. Tom and Jessie both threw their arms around her and held her close.

'You've been off getting your head together some-where haven't you honey?' Tom asked her. She smiled and nodded. 'We understand more than anyone your need for time and space, but please promise to let us know next time you disappear,' he scolded her.

'Message understood' she replied. 'I promise.'

Jessie left to make tea, while Tom and Melissa settled down into the deep comfortable chairs in the family room. She looked around at her surroundings. Nothing in the room matched, but still the room oozed warmth and security. Jessie returned with the tea moments later. Melissa waited until everyone's tea had been poured before speaking.

'I've given it a lot of thought these past few weeks, and I've decided to sell the apartment and go home.'

Tom and Jessie both looked at Melissa and then at each other. Tom spoke first.

'We understand. While your decision makes us sad, we're not surprised. We've been expecting you to get help or to leave for a while. The strain between yourself and Jonathan has been obvious in so many conversations.'

Jessie continued, 'We were relieved when you both decided to take some time out to re-evaluate your relationship and your life. You couldn't both go on silently destroying each other.'

Melissa was amazed by how clearly they had understood what was going on. She'd thought they'd been successfully keeping their private struggle to themselves. Obviously, not.

'I guess it'll take me a couple of weeks to sell the apartment and settle our affairs. I'd like to be able to be home in time to spend Christmas with Dad.'

A smile stretched across Melissa's face as she thought of her father and Christmas at home. She could almost smell the heady scent of eucalyptus and hear the cicadas' noisy chorus ringing through the valley. She hugged Tom and Jessie warmly and left.

As she unlocked the front door of the apartment, she heard the telephone ring. It was Jonathan's solicitors checking to see if everything was OK, because she had missed her appointment. Melissa apologised and made another appointment for the following morning. She then called a local real estate agency to arrange a time when they could meet to discuss the sale of the apartment. She looked at her watch and realised that it was probably too early to call her father in Australia. She tapped her foot impatiently, willing time to pass, and then picked up the telephone and dialled her father's number in Bangalow.

'George Bourne,' her father said slowly into the phone.

'Dad, it's me. I'm sorry to call you so early in the morning but ...'

'Darling, you know that you can call me anywhere, anytime,' he interrupted.

'Dad, I'm coming home.'

There was a pause on the other end of the phone.

'Dad?' she prompted.

'Oh darling that's so wonderful. This is your home, and this is where you should be, and this is where I can look after you,' he bubbled profusely into the phone.

She could hear him sniffing into a handkerchief.

'When will you be here?' he asked.

'As soon as I can get things settled here,' she replied. 'Christmas eve at the latest.'

'That's wonderful, just wonderful darling. This will be a good Christmas ... except,' her father paused suddenly remembering Jonathan's death.

'I know,' Melissa responded. 'I have to go now and

start packing. There's a lot to do but I'll call you again soon.'

'All right darling. I'll talk to you soon.'

Melissa hugged herself with delight as she hung up the phone. She surveyed the room, mentally noting the different kinds of packing cases she'd require. In the corner, still propped up against the divan, was Jonathan's open suitcase. On the floor beside the suit-case were the photos she'd been examining when Andrew knocked at the door. She picked the photos up and looked at them in greater detail. The smiling face was still a mystery to her. Melissa searched each of the inside pockets of the suitcase, hoping to find additional clues. There was nothing. She then started searching through the pockets of his clothes. They too were empty. She sat on the floor and stared at the case. On top of the books piled beside the suitcase was his wallet. She picked it up slowly and examined its contents, somewhat afraid of what she might find inside. Behind several twenty-dollar bills was a single sheet of paper.

Dearest Jonathan,

These past months have been the best.

I'm just writing to let you know that it's OK. I know why you can't leave Melissa and be with me. I know more than anyone in the world what it's like to be needed.

But I hope you understand why I can't stay. It hurts too much.

I won't be here when you come back. I've accepted a job in Vancouver so will be leaving tonight. Please don't follow me.

I'll always love you

Milly

Melissa read the letter again and then folded it up and put it back in the wallet. She was stunned. She had never suspected that there was somebody else in Jonathan's life. She walked into the study and started flicking through Jonathan's address book. There was no Milly listed anywhere. Feeling quite determined, she looked up Hank Matthews' phone number and dialled. Her hands were shaking as she listened to the phone ring.

'Hank? It's Melissa here,' she offered strongly.

'Oh, hello. How are you doing?' he replied cautiously.

'I want to talk to Milly.'

There was silence from Hank.

'I'm afraid that's not possible.'

'Look, Hank, I know everything, so it doesn't matter ...'

'Melissa,' Hank said gently, '... Milly is dead. She was in the car with Jonathan.'

'Dead?'

'I'm afraid so,' he replied softly.

Melissa remembered now about the second body

found in the wreckage. She'd been so shocked at the news of Jonathan's death that she'd forgotten about the other person in the car.

'Can you tell me about her?' she asked gently.

'Melissa ... even if I could tell you more, I'm not at all sure that's the best thing to do. Don't you want to let sleeping dogs lie and get on with your life?'

'Yes, I do want to get on, but I need to close a few doors first. I think that knowing more about Jonathan and Milly will help me do that.' She paused. 'Is there anyone else I could talk to?'

'Mmmm ... Well, if you're sure it's want you want. Her sister, Grace, lives in Boston too. I don't know her number, but her name is Grace Matheson. She might talk to you.'

'OK. I've got it. Thank you, Hank. Thank you for everything.'

It took her less than a minute to find G Matheson listed online and to dial the number.

'Hello,' was the simple reply of a woman on the other end of the line.

'Hello there. This is Melissa Brinkley speaking, Jonathan's wife.' Melissa offered boldly.

'Yes?' came the cautious reply.

'Are you Milly's sister?'

'Yes I am. What can I do for you Melissa?'

'Ahh ...' Melissa hesitated. 'Grace, I want you to help me to understand. I want you to tell me about Milly, and about Milly and Jonathan. I know it's a very big request. But please be reassured, it comes not from motives of anger or revenge but from a desire to better understand Jonathan. I'm not at all sure that I really knew him.'

'Are you free tomorrow?'

'Yes, I am,' Melissa replied quickly.

'OK. Why don't you meet me at the small café shop in Quincy Markets at ten tomorrow?'

Melissa stretched out on the divan and contemplated her day. She'd woken up tired and confused in hospital this morning, had sent Andrew away, found out she was going to have his baby, and that Jonathan had a lover, who'd been killed in the accident too. It was all too much to absorb. She wondered what else there could possibly be that she didn't know about his life. Melissa sighed, closed her eyes and rested her hands on her midriff, willing herself to feel the baby. She felt very alone. The grandfather clock in the hall chimed eight times. Melissa swung her legs off the divan, walked into her bedroom and collapsed into bed.

She was wide awake before the morning light came through the shutters. All night she had dreamed of Jonathan and Milly. As she waited for the dawn she was aware that she was very hungry. Thoroughly exhausted, she'd fallen asleep last night before she had eaten. She plodded into the kitchen and drank a litre of milk before finishing off a bread and butter pudding which Jessie had made for her.

It was a lovely clear day, which was unusual for December in Boston, and the Quincy Markets were crowded with tourists. When Melissa entered the cafe she immediately recognised Grace sitting in a corner booth. Grace shared her sister's fair skin and preference for short hair, but Melissa recognised her more because she was the woman who'd sat on her own in the back pew at Jonathan's funeral. Grace nodded at Melissa as she approached her table.

'I wasn't sure that you'd come, it is a brave thing to do.' Melissa knew immediately that she liked Grace.

'It's pretty brave of you to come and risk meeting a mad and bitter wife.' Melissa was smiling as she replied. It was the right thing to say. Grace returned her smile.

The waiter came with coffee and the two women were then left alone. For a few moments neither spoke, absorbed in their thoughts as they sipped their drinks. Grace interrupted the silence first.

'When you called me yesterday, you were so certain that I'd know all about Milly and Jonathan. What made you so sure of yourself?'

Melissa looked thoughtfully into her coffee cup and swirled around the coffee grinds lying in the bottom.

'I've never had a sister ... but I've always wanted one. I somehow imagined that sisters must be closer than any other members of the family, sharing all their secrets. That was why I felt so sure that you'd know about Jonathan.' Grace looked at Melissa but said nothing. She continued. 'Grace, please believe me when I say I'm very sorry about Milly. It must be very difficult, losing a sister, particularly one with whom you were close.'

Grace breathed in deeply and looked out into the passing crowd. She blinked, and tears ran down her face. Several minutes passed before Grace spoke.

'Yes. It has been very difficult. She's only been gone for a couple of weeks and I miss her terribly. I ache from the emptiness. I miss not being able to pick up the phone and have a chat; I miss her devilish sense of humour, I miss ... well I guess that I just miss everything about her. I really needed her. She gave me balance and perspective. In his own way, Jonathan needed her too.' Melissa leant forward and nodded gently, encouraging Grace to go on. 'Milly was a very strong person. Always sure of what she was doing and where she was going. People who could feel that strength, and those who needed that strength were attracted to her. I think that while Jonathan always appeared easy going and without a care in the world, he wanted reassurance, and reassurance and confidence came from being with Milly.'

Grace looked carefully at Melissa who was deep in thought.

'With you Melissa, it was different. I've no doubt Jonathan loved you, but I sense that it was more the protective love of a brother than that of a husband. He sometimes talked about when he first met you, how he was so attracted to your vulnerability. You seemed lost and hurt and in need of someone to look after you. So that's what he did. But in that brotherly role, Jonathan felt that he couldn't share his doubts with you because you needed him to be strong.'

'Oh Jonathan ... I understand ... if only I'd known,' Melissa whispered in a barely audible voice. Her attention returned to Grace. 'So what happened on the night of the accident?'

'I'm not sure exactly. Milly knew she'd created a conflict within Jonathan and the only way to resolve it was to leave. She told me she'd decided to end the relationship and go to Vancouver. I can only guess he found out she was leaving and convinced her to let him go too.'

Melissa remembered the letter she had found in Jonathan's suitcase and realised that what Grace had surmised was probably true. Melissa took a deep breath and sighed.

'Grace, I want to thank you so much for coming to meet with me today. It's made such a difference. I finally understand this gnawing tension that was eating away at Jonathan and destroying our marriage.'

'So, what are you going to do now?' Grace asked.

'Go home and start anew. I have a few broken fences to mend.'

'Well, good luck' said Grace

'Thank you,' replied Melissa, 'Thank you for everything.'

Grace collected her handbag and with a parting nod was gone. Melissa felt tired but free. Free because finally, nearly all the pieces in her life fitted together again. All the final pieces except one. That one piece was Andrew.

MID DECEMBER

*M*elissa met with a senior partner of Harris & Ryder, Attorneys at Law. Within two minutes of their meeting commencing that afternoon, he had informed her that she was the sole beneficiary of the worldly possessions of Jonathan Brinkley. Melissa thanked him for his services and left the offices ten minutes later. The speed with which Jonathan's estate was managed seemed to portend the speed with which all other events in Melissa's life suddenly took place. The apartment sold within forty-eight hours of being on the market, and all the furniture was bought by a local artist who had a passion for black leather and chrome. By the end of the third week in December, all that was left to do was to say goodbye to Jonathan's parents and a few friends.

It wasn't until Melissa had boarded the Qantas flight

for Los Angeles on the way to Sydney that she really felt she was going home. On the flight, all she could think of was Andrew. During the last week she had considered calling him. But each time she'd hung up before dialling the final few numbers. It was just too hard to tell him about the baby over the phone. She wasn't at all sure of how he felt about her since she had sent him away, nor how he would react to the news. It would be much easier if she told him herself.

As the plane flew in over Sydney Harbour, she looked out the window at the rows and rows of red roofed houses, and the shimmering blue swimming pools dotting so many Sydneysiders' back yards. She thought it funny that these two images so strongly represented the Australian lifestyle. Within minutes, she had landed and transferred to the domestic terminal where she caught her internal connection to Ballina.

George Bourne beamed as he saw his only child walk down the stairs from the plane. He carried a large bunch of proteas, waratahs and daisies, her favourite flowers. She couldn't help but blink back tears.

'G'day,' he said as he wrapped his arms around her, 'Welcome home.' Melissa revelled in the warmth of her father's embrace.

After dinner that night, Melissa knew she should wait no longer to share with her father her news.

'Dad.' Her father looked up at her. 'I'm going to have a

baby.' George seemed stunned, but quickly regained his composure.

'Oh darling ... that's wonderful, just wonderful. Won't Jessie and Tom be delighted?'

'I haven't told them. And I'm not sure when I will, because ...' Melissa paused and took a deep breath, 'because it isn't Jonathan's baby.'

'Mmm,' was all that George could respond after a moment's silence. He gingerly placed his hand on top of hers, leaned over, and kissed her on the forehead. Melissa knew everything would be OK.

The last three days before Christmas flew by. Melissa knew Andrew would be home to share Christmas dinner with his father and brothers, and looked forward to seeing him. But she was nervous. This would be the day that she'd tell him she loved him far more deeply than she'd realised. In her mind, she carefully planned what she would say to him and how he would react to her, and particularly to news of the baby.

Christmas day arrived hot and steamy. Melissa and her father shared a wonderful meal on the back veranda, soaking in the southerly breezes. On the home paddock fence, five kookaburras started a noisy chorus. Melissa looked to the sky and then to her father, 'I guess a storm is coming?'

'I reckon so,' he replied casually. 'I think if you're going to get over to the Wyatts' before it arrives, you'd better go now.'

She looked quizzically at her father, wondering if he'd guessed about Andrew.

'After all,' he continued, 'I don't think Charles would let me live it down if he didn't get his Christmas bucket of lychees.'

She smiled. The lychees, of course. It was now a well-established Christmas tradition for the Bournes to give the Wyatts a bucket of lychees from their local trees. In response, the Wyatts would give the Bournes a case of beautiful, bright orange mangoes. Both fruits were susceptible to the vagaries of weather and the tenacity of the local fruit bats. It was a competition between Charles and George to see who could deliver the best produce. Melissa picked up the small bucket of dark crimson lychees and headed off across the paddock and over the small bridge at Byron Creek. George watched his daughter until he could no longer see her, stretched and went inside for an afternoon snooze.

Melissa could hear laughter as she came closer to the Wyatt home. Perched on the front veranda sharing a joke were Miles and Neil Wyatt. They looked so much alike in terms of build and facial features. Both were stubbled from four days of not shaving. However, Miles was easily identifiable from a distance because his hair was uniquely blonde among the Wyatt men. Melissa enjoyed watching the companionship of the brothers without them being aware of her presence. As she cleared the blossoming crepe myrtle trees, Neil saw her and gave a shout. He swung his legs over the veranda rail, jumped down to the ground and gave Melissa a big hug. Miles was close behind and picked Melissa up and swung her round. It was all she could do not to scatter the lychees on the ground. 'Merry Christmas Melissa!' they both chimed in unison.

'When did you get home?' Neil asked.

'About a week ago now,' she replied.

'We didn't know you were coming. What a surprise, what a lovely surprise!' Neil offered with a smile. 'And do we have a surprise for you – guess who has gone and got himself engaged?'

Melissa smiled as she shrugged her shoulders.

'Andrew has. Can you believe it?'

'Engaged – Andrew?'

Melissa heard herself saying these words, but was overwhelmed with disbelief.

'Yeah,' Miles offered. 'All we know is he disappeared off the face of the earth for a few days in December, and then emerged again in a very sorry state. He refused to tell anyone where he'd been or what had happened. And then two weeks later he turns up here with Kate, and tells us all that they're getting married in June. Incredible, eh!'

'What's all this racket?' Charles Wyatt's voice boomed from the veranda.

'It's Melissa, Dad. She comes bearing gifts.' Neil had a huge grin on his face as he passed the bucket of lychees up to his father.

'Mmmm ...' Charles offered after he had examined the dozen or so lychees sitting at the top of the bucket in great detail.

'Not a bad crop I s'pose. Please thank your father, Melissa ... and Melissa ... there's a magnificent tray of mangoes on the kitchen table. Don't forget to take them with you when you go.'

'Thank you, Charles.' She reached up and kissed him on the cheek.

'Goodness. What is it about Christmas day that makes everyone so frisky?' he said. Melissa could see he was having difficulty not smiling.

There was a creaky sound on the veranda and she suddenly became aware of other listeners to their conversation. She looked up and saw Andrew standing silently in the far corner of the veranda next to a slim woman with dazzling russet curls.

'I think it would be good manners, son, if you introduced your fiancée to Melissa,' Charles said. Andrew and the woman walked over.

'Of course, Dad. My apologies, Melissa. Allow me to introduce Kate, Kate Williams.'

'Hello Melissa,' the young woman offered.

'Hello Kate. Nice to meet you.' she replied calmly. She surprised herself by her ability to disguise the turbulent way she was feeling. She knew she wouldn't be able to continue her calm charade for very long. She had to get away from here. She felt like a dam about to burst.

For a moment there hung a strange, uncomfortable silence over the group. A low distant grumble of thunder disturbed the impasse and turned everyone's attention to the western skies.

'There's a big storm coming,' Miles offered to no-one in particular.

'Melissa. Why don't you come inside for a Christmas drink and wait out the storm?' Neil offered.

'Thank you, Neil, but no. I think I'll leave now before the storm comes. And besides it's Christmas day, and I don't want to leave Dad alone for too long.'

A few heavy raindrops begin to fall from the ever-blackening sky and Melissa felt the tears swelling up behind her eyes, so turned to leave.

'I'll just go and get the mangoes for you, love,' Charles offered.

But she could wait no longer. Tears began to fall, and the storm opened up the floodgates. Melissa lifted up her skirt and ran down to the creek through the long grass. She was sobbing uncontrollably as she crossed the little bridge and ran towards the home paddock. The long grass was wet and slippery and she tripped and fell fifty metres from her father's house. A black crow sitting on the paddock gate screeched loudly. It was clearly afraid of the storm and warning anyone and anything that cared to listen. The bird flew off as Melissa reached the gate and she turned and watched the bird disappear into the distance. To Melissa, the bird suddenly symbolised a form of hope and now that hope was gone.

'Darling ... are you all right?' her father called out.

Melissa looked towards the house and could see her father on the back veranda. She waved, to show she was OK.

'What happened?' George asked.

Melissa wiped the tears from her eyes with the back of her hand.

'Oh, Dad. I went for a bit of a sixer near the bridge I'm afraid. It frightened the living day lights out of me. Could you get me the Dettol and plasters, please?'

George Bourne looked at his daughter's knees and then into her eyes. He suspected there was more to the tears than the grazed knees, but said nothing.

'Take a seat on the sofa and I'll get you a cuppa ... and something to clean up those battle scars,' he instructed.

Melissa was grateful for the tea. While her father cleaned and dressed her wounds, she said nothing. Outside the wind whipped around the lychee trees and the thundering rain turned the normally gurgling Byron Creek into a raging torrent. She could see out the window that the sky was dark and angry, occasionally punctuated by the brilliance of a lightning strike. With one loud clap of thunder, all the lights went out. While her father fumbled around in the cupboard looking for a torch,

Melissa listened to the orchestra of sounds the storm unleashed. She imagined being outside in the storm, running blindly through the rain trying to find home. Each time she thought she'd found the right path, Andrew stepped out from behind a tree and said, 'Melissa, I'd like to introduce you to Kate, Kate Williams.'

And she turned and ran in a different direction and there again he was, saying, 'Melissa, I'd like to introduce you to Kate, Kate Williams.'

She turned and ran to the bridge at Byron Creek. Just as she was about to cross the bridge she tripped and fell into the raging torrent. The flood waters drag her away from the bridge and from everything that was familiar to her. She was caught in a small whirlpool going round and around ... In the distance she heard voices. It was Andrew and he was calling to her,

'Melissa ... Melissa ... Melissa ...'

With a shudder she woke up from her dream. She realised she'd been asleep for some time – the storm had passed and although the electricity was still down, the house was awash with the grey light of early evening. In the darkness, she could hear her father talking to someone at the front door.

'Well, as long as she's alright then.'

'Yes, she'll be fine. It's only a graze. Thank you very much for your concern, and please thank your father for the mangoes.'

As Melissa's father walked back into kitchen the lights came on.

'Hello Sleeping Beauty. Are you feeling better now?'

'Yes, thanks Dad.'

'Young Andrew Wyatt was just here, checking to see you'd managed to get home all right. I said you were fine.' He paused before continuing. 'Are you going to go and see him?'

Melissa looked at her father then down at her hands which are now tightly clenched in her lap.

'I can't Dad. I can't ever. He's getting married.'

'Oh Melissa,' was all her father could say.

BOXING DAY – DECEMBER 26

*B*oxing Day arrived quietly. It was as though all the residents of Bangalow needed a day of solitude and peace after the high energy of Christmas day. Melissa drove her father's old Ford utility the fifteen kilometres to Byron Bay and selected a secluded spot on Clarkes Beach. She needed space and time to think.

The water of the Pacific Ocean was beautiful, clear and sparkling like broken crystal. Melissa gasped as she entered the gently lapping water which was cool today following the previous night's storm. Floating on her back in this vast expanse she felt safe and secure. All her problems drifted away. She daydreamed about being a seagull, soaring high over the ocean and around the headland, without a care. The seagulls looked so free, so wild and so at peace.

The sound of children laughing in the distance

roused her from her dreamy isolated world. Two small boys were building competing sand castles on the water's edge a little way up the beach. Curious as to the source of their jubilation, Melissa swam closer to investigate. Melissa smiled when she realised that the children were not only competing against each other to build the biggest castle but also against the incoming tide which was eroding their efforts with each wave.

'Scott, look,' one of the little boys screeched, 'there's a mermaid in the water.'

The little boy with the blond hair stopped shovelling sand on his castle and looked out to the water where his friend was pointing. His eyes opened wide.

'Mason, do you think she's lost?'

'Probably,' his friend replied knowingly.

The little boy called Scott ran into the ocean towards Melissa but cautiously stopped several metres away. His friend followed him.

'Where are you from?' Scott asked.

'Not really sure where my home is any more,' she replied honestly.

'Boy, that must be rough,' Mason chimed in helpfully.

'So ... what ... what are you just floating around here 'til you figure out where you're going?' Scott asked.

'I guess that's what I'm doing – just trying to find my place in the world.'

'But don't you have a home?'

'Well, sort of, but I need to find a new home and a new life,' she responded.

'You can always come to our home – you'd be very welcome.'

Melissa smiled, touched by his sincerity.

'Thank you. That's a lovely thing to say, but I think I need to find my own home.'

The boys nodded knowingly.

A call in the distance interrupts their conversation.

'That's Mum,' Scott told Melissa. 'We're going home. Are you sure you'll be able to find your way home?'

'I'm certain of it,' Melissa replied.

'OK then – bye.'

'Goodbye Scott, Goodbye Mason. Lovely to meet you. Thank you for coming out to say hello.'

There was another call in the distance – this time the voice was more impatient. The two boys turned towards shore and ran through the shallow water.

Melissa watched the two boys leave and suddenly felt calm. Everything'll be all right. I'll find a way to get my life back in order.

JANUARY

'I'll meet you there at 10:30 then. OK ... thanks Clyde.'

Melissa put her phone down.

'It's still available Dad,' she called out to her father in the kitchen.

'Well, if you're sure, you should go and have a look. But you mustn't take it unless it fully meets your needs.'

'Dad we've discussed this. I just can't stay here in Bangalow. You know there's no work and ... I can't risk bumping into ... and it's just too hard.'

Melissa's voice trailed off and an uncomfortable silence hung in the air.

Her father walked in from the kitchen and looked at his daughter. He said nothing but stroked the side of her face with his finger.

'It's OK darling. Just keep in touch and let me know how you're going. How both of you are going. And if it doesn't work out, you mustn't hesitate to come back home.'

Melissa nodded and walked back into her childhood bedroom to pack her bags.

There had been two items of interest in Brisbane's Saturday *Courier Mail*. The first was a small house for rent on Currumbin Creek at the back of the Gold Coast and the second was an interior designer's vacancy with a small firm at Elanora called Niche Design. Melissa had called Clyde Simmons at the real estate agency to arrange an inspection for Saturday morning and begun mentally preparing her application for the designer's position.

Melissa relaxed as she drove up the coast from Bangalow to Currumbin. Despite the fact that she had driven on this particular road hundreds of times, she never failed to marvel at the beauty of the changing countryside. In seventy-five kilometres she covered banana plantations, macadamia nut farms, and seaside holiday apartments. She arrived at the address provided at 10:15, and knew before she hopped out of the car that she'd arrived home. A small white timber cottage with a red corrugated tin roof sat nestled in a dazzling display of flowering trees, well back from the road. Two magnificent poinciana trees acted as natural umbrellas for the garden and house. In the trees, Melissa heard a cacophony of sounds as the local birds vied for each other's attention. A swarm of rosellas dived into the heart of a bottlebrush tree and cried out together in a noisy chorus.

She walked around the side of the house through a kaleidoscope of impatiens and down to where the lush green grass touched the creek bed. An old timber swing for two swayed gently in the breeze from the bough of an enormous jacaranda tree. Melissa sat on the swing and sighed.

'What a magical place,' she thought.

Heavy footsteps on the grass interrupted her tranquil spell.

'Melissa Brinkley?'

Clyde Simmons was a bear of a man who Melissa guessed, judging by his size, probably enjoyed too much amber liquid and good food.

'Would you like to have a look inside?'

Melissa nodded and followed the burly real estate agent up the back steps and into the timber cottage.

'Can I move in today?' she asked as they walked in to the kitchen.

'Don't you want to see the rest of the house first?' he replied, before turning, smiling and throwing her a set of keys.

❧

Within a week Melissa began to feel like she'd always lived in the cottage on Currumbin Creek. Her father had given her a few pieces of furniture, which reminded her of Bangalow. She obtained the designer's position at Elanora, a six-month contract to cover an employee on maternity leave. This amused her. Given the short-term nature of the contract, there was no immediate need to reveal her pregnancy to her employers. However, she needed to consider future income. A partial solution arrived on her first day at work when she overheard an architectural student, Ben, being given a last warning for being late. She caught up with him by the coffee machine and learnt he was battling the traffic from Brisbane each day.

'I have a spare room in my house – five kilometres away on Currumbin Creek. It's available for a reasonable price.' Melissa offered. Ben's face brightened.

'Can I take a look this afternoon?' he replied quickly.

Melissa wrote down the address for him. She looked at Ben a little more closely as she handed him the paper. He was tall, with a sandy coloured fringe that frequently fell over his left eye. A rich sprinkling of freckles over the bridge of his nose suggested many days spent in the sun. He was lean and muscular.

'You're a surfer?' Melissa asked.

'How'd you know?' Ben replied.

'Stab in the dark,' she offered with a smile.

❦

At half past five there was a knock on her front door.

'I'll take the room,' Ben blurted out before the door was fully open.

'You haven't seen the room yet,' Melissa cautioned.

'Don't care. It's five minutes to the beach, ten minutes to the office and twenty-five minutes to Uni. I'm in heaven. But I'll have a look at the room.'

'Here tis,' Melissa pointing to the door immediately to her left.

Ben walked in, frowned, and adopted a Perry Mason inspired position with his arms. He undertook a mini circuit of the room, letting his eyes run over the bed, wardrobe and desk.

'Hmmmm yes. This will be acceptable,' he said turning to Melissa, smiling broadly.

'Now, there's one more thing you need to know before you accept.' Melissa added. 'You need to know we'll have company.'

'A boyfriend,' Ben proposed playfully.

'No. A baby. I'm having a baby in August. But I'm not telling work yet, so can you keep it to yourself?'

Ben's eyebrows shot skyward.

'No worries. Fine with me, Mel. Can I call you that? You'll make a great mum.'

Melissa smiled. 'When can you move in?'

'Is tomorrow too early?'

Melissa laughed and handed him a front door key. 'Let me show you the rest of the house.'

FEBRUARY

*M*elissa entered the third month of her pregnancy, enjoying the work at Niche Design, and her life with Ben. Client meetings took her up and down the coast from Brisbane to Ballina, giving her opportunity to enjoy driving around the Gold Coast while noting the arrival of autumn. Her clothes were feeling a little snug and at the ten-week mark, she cried when she heard the baby's heart beat for the first time in the doctor's surgery. Her pregnancy instantly became very real. While she didn't suffer from morning sickness, she did have wild dreams, typically involving Andrew. He was never far from her thoughts. Her father gently suggested that she tell him about the baby. But she hesitated, replying that it was still too early.

April brought showers and an important milestone. At the next doctor's appointment, it might be possible to determine the baby's gender. The day arrived and the clock on the office wall moved excruciatingly slowly towards 5:00pm. She was in her car as the clock's hands reach the designated hour. Not surprisingly she arrived at the surgery early, but the doctor was running half an hour late. She groaned and flipped through the dog-eared copies of the *Australian Women's Weekly* without interest. The waiting room was full of excited couples, whispering softly. She suddenly felt very alone.

'Mrs Brinkley?' the nurse announced.

'I'm here' Melissa replied.

'Alone today?' the nurse enquired.

Melissa nodded and followed her into the doctor's office.

She settled on to the examination lounge and examined the doctor's face carefully as he watched the screen and ran the ultrasound wand over her belly.

'Hmm,' he murmured several times. 'Your baby is looking good. Yes, he's looking very good Melissa.'

'He?' Melissa whispered, as the tears started to well up in her eyes.

A son. She had a son. Andrew's son.

Melissa beamed.

Unbeknown to her, while Melissa was at the doctor's office, Andrew had called round to her house. He knocked tentatively on the door and was surprised when Ben appeared.

'Yep?' Ben asked.

'Ahh,' Andrew fumbled. 'I was hoping to see Melissa.'

'She's not home yet,' Ben offered simply.

'Ahh,' Andrew replied. He looked at Ben more closely. 'Who are you?'

'I'm Ben,' he replied a little indignantly.

'And you ... ?' Andrew hesitated, unsure of what he was asking.

'Live here,' Ben replied

'Ahh,' Andrew repeated. He was momentarily lost for words.

'Can you tell Melissa I called,' he asked.

'And who are you?' Ben enquired.

'I'm Andrew Wyatt ... her ... her old neighbour from Bangalow. In fact, her father asked me to drop off this fruit.' He passed the box of quinces and pomegranates to Ben.

'Super,' Ben replied eyeing the beautiful fruit. 'Do you want to wait for her inside?'

'No. Well, no. Um. I'll call her later. Thanks again,' Andrew gushed nervously and with this rushed signoff he walked to his car and reversed out of the driveway.

Ten minutes later, a still-teary Melissa arrived home.

Ben was in the kitchen when he heard her key in the front door. He walked to the end of the hall to watch the door open.

'Cup of tea in the garden? he suggested, not knowing what else to say. She smiled and went to the bathroom to wash her face.

While Melissa was in the bathroom, Andrew was driving back to her. He made it as far as Tugun, before deciding to turn around. He wasn't sure what message Ben, whoever he was, would leave. And he really wanted to speak with her. He missed her. He had so much to say, and more than three months had passed since that awkward exchange on Christmas day.

He could see her car in the driveway, so parked his on the street and walked slowly up the driveway. His knocks on the front door, went unanswered. He could hear voices so walked around the side of the house. A small screech made him run to the corner where he saw Melissa hugging Ben.

'So that answers that question,' he said softly to himself. He turned, walked quietly back to the car and drove away.

Ben released Melissa from his enthusiastic embrace and looked again at the ultrasound photo.

'No denying that's a baby.'

'Yes, and quite a bouncy one,' she chipped in. 'A beautiful, bouncy baby boy.'

'You know, you're going to have to come clean soon. You won't be able to hide it much longer.'

'I know.' She picked up their tea cups, walked back inside into the kitchen and noticed the box of fruit on the corner counter as she placed the cups in the sink. 'Where'd you get the fruit from?' she called out through the kitchen window.

'Oh crikes. Forgot. It's from your dad.'

'I missed my dad today? Why didn't you tell me? I must call him.'

'No, no ... not your Dad. Delivered by one of his neighbours.'

'Who was it?' Melissa asked softly.

Ben hesitated. 'I think it was... Wyatt? Someone Wyatt'

'And a first name?' she prodded.

'Hmmm. Forgot. Should have written it down. Sorry,' he replied sheepishly. 'Why don't you call your dad? He'll know who it was.'

Melissa reached for her phone and walked towards the back door.

'Andrew,' Ben suddenly blurted out. 'It was Andrew.'

Melissa stopped and closed her eyes.

'He'd been here today!' So close. Melissa imagined she could feel his presence. She continued to the garden, sat on the swing and pressed speed dial number one. Her father answered the call four rings later. He was moving more slowly these days. 'Dad, I have news,' she chirped.

'Let me guess. You've received a box of the season's best quinces and pomegranates?'

'Absolutely. They're on the kitchen bench and they're beautiful. But that's not all.'

'Yes' he replied tentatively. 'Go on'.

'I've a photo of your grandson.'

There was silence in Bangalow. George Bourne was lost for words.

'A son,' he whispered. 'How wonderful. And how did Andrew react to the news?'

This time there was silence in Currumbin.

'I wasn't here when he called, Dad.'

'Perhaps you could call him now?'

'I don't think this is a conversation we should have over the phone. But soon, in person, I promise I'll tell him.'

'All right then.'

'Love you Dad. Talk soon.'

Melissa finished the call and walked back inside. She stopped at the room that she'd been using as a study. It would now need to be converted into a nursery for her son.

MAY

*W*inter arrived in May allowing Melissa to continue to hide her expanding waist-line under baggy jumpers. She knew she wouldn't be able to keep the pregnancy a secret much longer, but she was not ready for the inevitable questions about the father and how she'd manage on her own. While others weren't aware of her condition, she certainly was, as the baby's energetic kicks were ever present.

A client in Byron Bay provided an opportunity to combine work with a visit to her father in early June. Her morning in The Bay was spent visiting the client's house near Wategos beach and in meeting with planners at Byron Shire Council. Meetings wrapped up with hand-shakes and hugs after a boisterous lunch at the Beach Byron Bay restaurant. It had been a successful visit, but Melissa was tired. She looked to the sky as she walked to her car. Dark clouds were approaching quickly from the north. It was only fifteen kilometres to Bangalow, but the approaching *Queen's Birthday* long weekend would mean that the roads were busy. Melissa called her father to let him know that she was on her way. Heavy raindrops started falling as she took the main road out of town.

Her father put the phone back on the kitchen bench and frowned. He walked out to the veranda to check the blackening sky. Experience told him that the storm would be fast and furious. The grandfather clock in the hallway chimed three times. George looked at his watch to double check the time. There was a distant rumble of thunder. He walked inside and nervously set the table for dinner. Heavy rain started to fall. Ten minutes later it was replaced by the clattering of hail on the tin roof. The sound was deafening, like marbles on a glass-top table. The lights went out and George scrambled to find the torch in the kitchen pantry. A thin pole of light pierced the darkness. Gravel crunching on the driveway filled him with relief. She'd arrived. He collected a large umbrella from the laundry and rushed to the front door.

'I was worried about you,' he called out.

'And I was worried about you,' Andrew replied as he shook off his raincoat. 'I thought you might need help getting your generator started.'

'Oh, Andrew. I thought you were Melissa. She's not here yet. I'm worried with the traffic in this storm. Come in, come in.'

He wiped his feet and George closed the door behind him. The storm was getting weaker and moving south. The lights flickered on.

Andrew turned to George and could see the concern in his face.

'Call her. She might just be stuck in traffic.'

George pressed the speed dial on his phone. After three rings, he heard his daughter's cheery voice instructing him to leave a message. His eyes swelled with tears.

'Voice mail?' Andrew asked.

He nodded.

'Turn on local TV,' Andrew instructed.

'We interrupt local programming to advise of a multi-car pileup on Ewingsdale Road. Emergency crews are on site. Details of the storm and its impact coming up next.'

'I'll drive, George. Central Hospital is where they'll take any casualties.'

Andrew passed George his coat and opened the front door. George walked on to the veranda in a daze. Andrew took the keys from the bowl on the nearby stand, and locked the door. Neither spoke. They listened to the radio for further updates.

'There has been extensive damage to crops and tailbacks of traffic. Wreckage from a multi-car pileup in Byron Bay has now been cleared. The storm cell continues to move south bringing strong winds and torrential downpours to Yamba. In other news ...'

Andrew turned the radio off. George called Melissa again, only to reach her voice mail. He hung up and put the phone back in his top pocket.

'Leave a message. Let her know we're on our way.'

George called again and waited for the beep.

'Hi Melissa. It's Dad. Bit worried about you, what with the wet and the traffic. We're coming down to....' George hesitated. '...to The Bay. Just call me when you get this. Love you.'

George put the phone back in his pocket and put his head in his hands. Andrew put his hand on George's knee for a moment, before returning it to the steering wheel. As they exited the Hinterland highway they passed a tow truck parked beside the road. With horror, they both saw Melissa's badly crumpled car.

With his heartbeat racing, Andrew pulled into Byron Central Hospital car park. He helped the badly shaken George out of the car and into the hospital reception which was swarming with people.

'Wait here. I'll see if they have any news.'

George collapsed into a seat and rested his head in his hands while Andrew joined a queue at the reception desk.

'Cup of tea, sir?'

George looked up to see a woman, holding out a steaming cup of tea. She had a badge that said 'volunteer' on her lapel. He nodded, took the tea and whispered 'thank you.' She sat down beside him. 'I'll wait with you until your son returns.'

'He's not my...' George hesitated, '.... He's my neighbour. We're trying to find my daughter.'

The woman nodded. 'You must be very anxious.'

Tears streamed down George's face.

She passed him a handkerchief and he wiped his tears before taking another sip. He could see Andrew had made it to the front of the queue and was having a conversation with the receptionist. George stood and the woman took the cup from his shaking hands. He finished the conversation and walked towards them both. George searched Andrew's face for any sign of emotion. It revealed nothing.

'She's here,' he said simply. 'She's in surgery. That's all they could tell me. Let's go to the waiting room near theatre to wait for the doctor.'

'Well, you've found her and she's in good hands. I'll show you where the waiting room is,' the kindly woman offered.

'Thank you,' Andrew said to the woman. 'Who are you?

'I'm Helen, and I'm a volunteer at the hospital.'

'Thank you, Helen,' Andrew replied, 'and this is George, Melissa's father.'

She nodded and led them down a hall to the waiting room. They had no sooner taken their seats in the corner when a doctor entered the room.

'Mr Brinkley?' she enquired.

They all stood, nervously looking at each other.

'I'm Mr Bourne, Melissa's father,' George responded.

Helen excused herself and moved to join a family on the other side of the room.

'Sit. Please sit,' the doctor instructed.

Andrew and George sat down.

She turned to Andrew and asked, 'You are?'

'I'm a neighbour, I'm a friend of the family ... '

'It's OK. He can hear what you have to say, Doctor,' George offered.

'She's very lucky,' the doctor started. 'That was a terrible accident and she's been saved from worse injuries by the airbag.'

Worse ... played over in Andrew's head.

'She's sustained major lacerations, extensive bruising and trauma to the head. The impact of the collision prompted early labour and we had to deliver the baby by caesarean section. Mother and son are now both in intensive care.'

Startled, Andrew looked at George but said nothing.

'They are in a serious condition. We'll know more in a few hours.'

'Is it possible to see her? George asked quietly.

'Yes, but only family, and only one person at a time. And please keep the visit brief.'

He nodded.

'I'll wait for you here George.'

They walked out of the waiting room together and Andrew watched as the doctor took George to intensive care. He was about to return to the waiting room when he heard a shout from an adjacent corridor and watched two nurses pass, pushing a tiny life form in a humidicrib. The baby was in respiratory distress.

Tears welled up in Andrew's eyes. He returned to the waiting room and slumped into a seat in the corner. His head was full of questions. A baby. Melissa had a baby?

His phone ringing broke into his reflections. He looked at the screen and saw that it was Kate.

'Is that my missing-in-action fiancée by chance? Where are you honey? Your father says dinner is thirty minutes from being on the table.'

'I'm at the hospital.'

'With George? Is he OK?' Kate enquired.

'Yes, I'm with George, but he's fine, well, kind of, it's Melissa. There's been an accident. Kate sorry – can you put Dad on the line?'

The line went silent for a few seconds. Andrew could hear Kate's footsteps across the timber kitchen floor.

'What's happened?' Charles asked quickly.

Andrew explained about the accident and how they found Melissa and described her current condition. He omitted to mention the baby.

'Goodness, son. What can I do?'

'Can you come and take George home and stay with him tonight? He's in shock and I'm worried about him. I'll stay here and come home tomorrow when you bring George back.'

'Of course. Traffic permitting, I'll be there in half an hour.'

'Thanks Dad.'

'Do you want to speak to Kate again?'

Andrew hesitated. 'Put her on Dad.'

'Are you OK honey?' Kate asked softly.

'I'm all over the place Kate. I won't be home tonight. I'm going to stay at the hospital. Dad can update you. I'll call you tomorrow,' he replied quickly.

Kate hesitated. 'I'll come to the hospital to be with you.'

'No Kate. Stay there. We'll speak tomorrow.' He paused then quietly added 'Bye.'

'Bye,' Kate replied.

Andrew hung up before he could hear Kate add, 'love you.'

*

Andrew heard footsteps and saw George returning to the waiting room.

'How is she?' he asked.

'Impossible to tell. She's still unconscious and covered in bandages. The nurse tells me we need to wait and see. Her body needs rest.'

'And so do you. You've had a big shock and there's

nothing more that can be done now. You need to go home, and rest.'

'I can't leave her Andrew. If she wakes up and no-one's here ...' George caught his breath.

'I'll be here. I'll take the first shift and will call you if there's any change. I promise.'

George sighed. He felt weary and looked at his watch. Eight o'clock.

He looked into Andrew's eyes, but said nothing. Footsteps in the corridor distracted them.

'George, Andrew, how is she?' Charles asked anxiously.

'No change yet Dad, but she's receiving good care.'

At that moment the attending doctor walked towards them. She addressed herself to George.

'She's resting and her vital signs are stable. These are good things. We'll know more tomorrow. Go home and rest.'

'Can I visit her now Doctor ... Doctor McDonald?' Andrew asked looking at her name badge.

The doctor looked at George for approval.

He nodded. 'He's family.'

The doctor acknowledged the comment, and Andrew turned to George.

'George, Dad is here to take you home and he'll bring you back tomorrow. I promise I'll call if there's any change.'

He nodded and Charles buttoned up his jacket for

him. He put his arm around his neighbour and led him out of the hospital.

Andrew watched them leave and then walked to the intensive care unit with the doctor.

Machines were beeping very softly and there was a strong smell of hospital disinfectant. Andrew gasped when he saw Melissa. She looked so frail. The doctor pointed Andrew to the chair by her bed and left to speak to the attending nurse. Andrew pulled the chair closer and reached out to hold her hand. It was cold, limp and soft. He kissed it and breathed in the scent of her. Memories of their time together in Brisbane played softly in his head.

Andrew heard the doctor saying goodnight to the nurse. She approached the bed and placed a blanket over his knees.

'I suspect you'll need this.' The doctor smiled.

'Thank you' Andrew replied. 'Very thoughtful.'

The doctor turned to leave.

'Doctor?'

'Yes.'

'How is the baby?'

'In a serious condition. He was born very early and the shock of the accident ...' Her voice trailed off.

'How early was he?'

The doctor looked at Andrew and hesitated. Family members typically know this information.

'Difficult to say,' she replied simply. 'We have called

the NETS[1] newborn emergency team for advice and possible helicopter evacuation of the baby to another hospital. Hopefully they'll be here soon. Good night.'

And with that, the doctor turned and left.

Andrew was now alone with Melissa. He watched the shallow rising of her chest, and glanced at the monitors beside the bed. Rising slowly, he reached over and kissed her gently on the forehead. He settled back into the chair and pulled the blanket up to his shoulders. Andrew had a fitful night's sleep. At 5:00am, he woke shivering as the blanket had fallen on the floor. He smiled at the nurse who checked Melissa's vital signs and wrote up her observations.

The nurse signalled for Andrew to follow her outside.

'She's stable. I think that we may move her into another ward today.'

That's good news' Andrew replied. 'And her son?'

She hesitated.

'No change I'm afraid. We all need to wait. The first twenty-four hours are critical.'

'Can I see him?'

'Of course. Follow me.'

The nurse led Andrew down the corridor to a special care ward. The little boy was on his side in a humidicrib.

He had dark hair peeking out from beneath a blue striped bonnet.

'Can I touch him?'

'We'll ask the doctor later,' she replied.

'May I?' Andrew asked, holding up his phone as a signal to take a photo.

Again, the nurse hesitated. 'No flash and quickly.'

Andrew took one photo and thanked the nurse.

She escorted him out and he signalled he was going to get coffee.

He walked down the empty corridor lost in his thoughts. The coffee from the machine was awful but it helped him feel more awake. He walked outside into the crisp winter morning and shivered. Cows mooing in the distance were on their way to the milking shed. Traffic was already building up on the main road. Andrew looked at his watch and remembered his promise to keep George aware of any changes in Melissa's condition.

George answered the phone on its second ring.

'Good news, George. The nurse thinks they'll be able to move Melissa out of intensive care today.'

'Wonderful. And the boy?'

'No change.'

'Oh,' is all George could say. He paused. 'Your dad and I will be there shortly.'

'OK. See you both soon.'

Andrew was suddenly hungry. He walked out to his car, and pulled a Kit-Kat from the glove box. The sweet chocolate helped remove the bitter flavour of the coffee. He turned on the radio. *Ain't No Sunshine When She's Gone* was playing. The feelings of nostalgia and regret resonated. The song ended and he sat alone in the car with his thoughts until his father's jeep pulled up alongside him thirty minutes later.

He got out of the car and hugged both men.

His father spoke first. 'George, you go in and see Melissa. I'll be in the waiting room.'

George nodded and walked into the hospital.

Charles turned to face Andrew.

'Have you called Kate yet?'

Andrew shook his head.

'Go home now. You have a wedding in two weeks and an anxious bride-to-be at home.'

'But ...' Andrew started.

'No buts Andrew. Go.'

Charles patted his son on the back and walked into the hospital.

Andrew returned to his car and put on his seatbelt. He sat there for a moment before firing the ignition and heading back to Bangalow.

JUNE 9 – MORNING

Kate was sitting at the kitchen table when Andrew got home.

'How is she?' Kate asked.

'Stable,' he replied. He walked behind her and rubbed her back.

'Did you get much sleep?'

'Some,' he replied. 'I'm OK.'

Andrew walked to the fridge and poured himself a glass of milk. He drank it slowly, staring out the kitchen window.

'So, what's next?' Kate asked.

'Don't know.' He washed out the glass and turned it upside down on the sink.

'I'm going to shower, change my clothes and go back to the hospital.'

'Andrew. We've loads of things to arrange for the

wedding. Her father is at the hospital. Your father's there. Do you really need to be there too?'

Andrew turned and looked at Kate. Her face was drawn and pale. She clearly had only had a few hours of sleep as well.

'I'm sorry Kate. I do.'

Silence hung between them.

'I'll try to be back for lunch. That's all I can say now.'

She nodded and said nothing. Andrew walked to the bedroom to get his clothes and moments later was is in the shower. As the warm water hit his body, he felt overwhelmed, and tears streamed down his face. He dried himself, dressed, and walked back out to the kitchen to collect his car keys. Kate hadn't moved from her chair. He walked over to her and kissed her on the cheek.

'I'll call later. I promise.'

'Will you?' Kate demanded, surprisingly strong.

Andrew was shaken by her change in tone.

'Should I cancel the wedding?' she added.

Andrew looked out the window and didn't respond. His phone rang. He looked at the number, pressed the green button, and then looked at Kate.

'Dad?'

'It's the baby, Andrew,' his father whispered, 'come back to the hospital.'

Andrew didn't remember the drive back to Byron Bay. He felt guilty at having left Melissa that morning, and now at having walked out on an unfinished conversation with Kate. He screeched into the carpark and ran inside. George and his father were talking to the doctor, huddled in a corner of the reception area. They look up as Andrew approached and pulled a spare plastic chair closer. Andrew sat, carefully examining their faces.

'The baby?' Andrew asked softly.

'He's dying. They have moved him and Melissa into their own room. He's not expected to last the day.' Charles put his hand gently on his son's shoulder.

'And Melissa ...?'

'She's still unconscious,' George said softly. 'We're discussing what to do.'

'She'd want to see her son. We must try to wake her,' Andrew said.

'Agreed,' he replied. The doctor nodded made a note on her clipboard and stood up.

Andrew and George followed her into Melissa's room. The baby was in the humidicrib in the corner being attended by a nurse. Andrew leant over Melissa and kissed her forehead.

'Melissa, can you hear me?' He stroked her arm. 'You have a son who wants to meet you.'

Melissa's fingers twitched.

Andrew looked at George and then at the nurse.

'Can we bring him over here?'

The nurse nodded. She removed him from the humidicrib and passed him to George. He rocked the tiny infant saying nothing.

'Hey Grandpa,' Andrew said with tears in his eyes.

George was crying too.

He walked slowly to the bed with his precious cargo.

'Melissa honey. It's Dad. I have a special bundle in my hands.'

Melissa's eyes flickered and slowly opened. She turned her head. It hurt.

'Dad.'

'Hello, sleeping beauty. I have someone here who would like to meet you.'

Melissa closed her eyes again. She must be dreaming. Her head was throbbing. She smelt disinfectant and was confused.

'Honey, it's Dad,' her father whispered.

Melissa heard a whimper like a kitten and lay very still to focus on the sound.

Someone was stroking her left arm. She opened her eyes a little again and looked at her arm. The hand was familiar. She moved her head slightly to the left and saw Andrew.

Her fingers stroke the bed linen and she felt the starch crispness of the hospital's cotton sheets. They were not familiar.

I'm in bed and I'm dreaming, she murmured in her head as she closed her eyes.

Again, she heard the sound of a kitten mewing.

Ohhh. Gotta wake up and help that kitten. Ohhh. I hurt. There's something on top of me. What is it? Get it off, she screamed inside her head.

Melissa moved her body and became aware of pain, intense pain and not just in her head, but in her neck, her arms, her shoulders and her stomach. She moved her hand to her stomach and suddenly remembered the baby. She opened her eyes with a start, remembering the deafening crunching of metal and the shattering of glass. Someone was sitting on her bed. She turned her head to the right and saw her father's tired eyes.

'Dad? Are you OK?'

'Hello there. Welcome back. I have someone here who would like to meet you.'

Melissa could see a blue striped bonnet poking out from a bundle of white blankets.

She looked closely and saw a tiny, clenched fist. Her father moved the bundle nearer and she saw a baby's face. She started crying.

'He's beautiful.'

'Yes, ten fingers and ten toes and an impressive mop of black hair under that bonnet.'

'Hello there little one. I've been waiting for you.'

Melissa stroked his face.

'He's so early. He's so tiny. Is he OK?'

Melissa suddenly remembered seeing Andrew. She

turned her head slowly to the left and looked at his face. He smiled.

'You forgot to shave this morning,' she observed smiling slightly. 'How long have I been here?' she asked him. 'What day is it?'

Andrew reached out and held her hand.

'It's Saturday, and you were in a car accident yesterday.'

Melissa concentrated hard but could only remember the sound of hail pounding on her car's bonnet.

The baby spluttered and Melissa turned back to her father.

'Do you want to hold your son?' he asked.

Melissa nodded and the nurse came over to help lift her to a sitting position with pillows arranged behind her back.

George passed the baby to his daughter and Andrew pressed the video button on his phone. Tears ran down Melissa's face. She examined his tiny clenched fists and kissed his nose, breathing in the scent of him He was so soft and fragile. His eyelashes fluttered for a moment and then he was still. Andrew turned off the video on his phone.

'He's not moving,' Melissa cried out and the doctor rushed over to examine the tiny body, that had exhausted his life.

'I'm sorry Mrs Brinkley. He's gone.'

Melissa let out a deep wail and started sobbing

uncontrollably. Her father tried to hold her but she was inconsolable. The nurse moved to close the door so as not to disturb other patients and Andrew heard the doctor telling her to get sedatives. He also heard her whispering to the nurse to record the time of death of 'baby boy Brinkley' as 9:25am, Saturday June 9.

Andrew felt numb. It was all so final and so unfair.

Melissa was now holding the little boy's body close to her chest and rocking gently. She could no longer feel the pain of her battered body. It was the loss of her beautiful, perfect son that was breaking her heart.

Sedatives were administered into Melissa's IV tube and she became calmer. Andrew and her father helped her settle back down into bed, still clutching the baby's body.

'We'll leave you alone for a bit,' the doctor whispered in Andrew's ear. Andrew mouthed 'thank you', and the doctor and nurse left.

George stroked his daughter's hair lovingly.

'I am so sorry, darling.'

He kissed her on the forehead, and gave Andrew a hand signal that he was going for a walk. He left the room moving slowly, like a broken man.

Andrew took off his shoes and climbed on to the single bed, embracing Melissa and their son. Melissa was losing the battle to stay awake. She barely acknowledged Andrew's presence as her gaze remained fixed on the baby. Ten minutes later she fell asleep. Andrew lay still and held them both close, soaking in the sadness. He was aware that the door opened and George stepped in. He looked at Andrew and nodded, acknowledging the intimate moment, and then quietly left, closing the door behind him. Andrew climbed off the bed and put his shoes on. He went around to the other side of the bed and untangled the baby from Melissa's arms. His face looked peaceful and Andrew imagined that he was only sleeping. He held the baby close, for just a moment. The door opened and Doctor McDonald entered. Andrew kissed the baby, took the little blue bonnet from his head and carefully put him back into the humidicrib. The doctor pushed the humidicrib beside Melissa's bed, and walked quietly to the door.

'We'll leave the baby with you both for a while before taking him away. I know that this is difficult, but when George is ready, I can arrange for someone to talk to him about registering the boy's birth and death, and organising an appropriate funeral. And we have counsellors on hand.'

'Thank you, Doctor. I will let George know.'

Andrew walked to the visitors' waiting room and saw George sitting beside Helen, sipping a cup of tea. She looked up as Andrew approached.

'I see that you have company, Mr Bourne. I'll come around later to see how you are.'

'Lovely woman,' George offered to Andrew as she left the waiting room.

Andrew took the seat vacated by Helen.

'Where's Dad?'

'Home. I told him to go home and that I'd call him if I needed a ride. Helen has a car and has offered to be my driver if needed.'

Andrew nodded and felt a little lighter at this unexpected friendship.

'She's asleep now, and I suspect will be for some time. When you are ready, the doctor wants to talk with you about arrangements for the baby.'

George nodded.

'I'm going back to Dad's place now but I'll come back later. Call me if you need anything.'

'Thank you, son,' he said.

Andrew was momentarily taken aback by the familiar way in which George addressed him.

He nodded, stood up and walked out to the hospital car park where he called Kate to let her know he was on his way back to Bangalow.

※

Kate was laying the table for lunch when Andrew walked in the front door. The house had a comforting smell of lamb infused with rosemary and roasting vegetables. There were six place settings and Andrew suddenly remembered that a family pre-wedding lunch had been planned for the Saturday of the long weekend. He walked over to Kate and kissed her on the cheek. She didn't move her face to receive his lips and continued to walk around the table laying the dinner plates. Tyres on the gravel driveway announced the arrival of visitors.

'Ahoy there,' came a cheery call from the front door. Miles, Neil and William Wyatt walked in together laden with wine and flowers. They patted Andrew on the back and kissed Kate.

'Where's Dad?' Miles asked Andrew.

He shrugged his shoulders and looked to Kate.

'Just picking up fresh bread in town. Back shortly.'

'And speaking of the devil,' Miles declared as Charles strode purposefully into the kitchen, and stared unloading bread and cakes on the bench.

It was clear to Andrew that his brothers were unaware of the accident. He sighed and suddenly noticed how hot he felt. He started unbuttoning his jacket and the blue striped bonnet fell out of his inside pocket onto the kitchen table. Andrew scooped it up quickly and put it back in his coat. He hung his coat on the rack in the hall.

'What's that?' William asked.

Andrew looked at the beautiful lace tablecloth which had been his mother's favourite. He looked at his father who cleared his throat.

"There's been an accident, boys. A car crash, yesterday afternoon at The Bay. And I am going need your assistance now to support George Bourne, who is not in a good way.'

'Oh no,' said Neil, shocked, 'not George.'

'No. No. It's not George, it's Melissa. Melissa had the accident and has sustained extensive injuries. She's in the Central, and receiving good care. George, on the other hand ... he hardly enjoyed a strong constitution before this. He's rattled and he's tired. If we can all do something small, that will leave him free to help Melissa through this.'

'What do you suggest Dad?' Miles asked.

'Well, I've been thinking ... Miles, you can check his cattle once a week? Just to make sure all is OK. William, can you slash the home paddock once a fortnight. Neil if you could manage the weekly grocery shop. And Andrew, perhaps you could follow up with the insurance company about Melissa's car. There'll be a claim to be made and you should be able to manage that easily enough from Brisbane.'

The brothers nodded. There was silence.

'But what about the baby bonnet?' William asked again.

'She was pregnant,' Andrew started. 'The impact of the accident brought on early labour so the baby was delivered by caesarean section. The child, the little boy,' Andrew hesitated 'did not survive.'

'Goodness,' William said softly. 'How awful. That's just not fair. She's lost her husband and now their son.'

The timer on the oven screamed loudly, piercing the tension in the room. Kate put the oven mitts on and took the lamb and vegetables out of the oven. Andrew moved to the kitchen to help her while his brothers left the room to wash their hands. Charles placed jugs of water on the table and arranged the flowers in a vase. No one spoke until everyone was seated.

'A sad day,' Charles started, 'a day to remember friends and family and how much they mean to us. Always thinking of you, Emily. Thank you for this beautiful meal, Kate. Thank you everybody for being here. Please eat.'

For the next hour the discussion around the table returned to the familiar pattern of grain prices and expected rainfall. Kate and Andrew said very little, lost in their private thoughts.

'Let's serve cake on the veranda,' Charles suggested once the dinner plates had been cleared.

The winter sunshine warmed the timber on the back veranda and the cushions on the rattan lounges. Andrew sank into their warmth and looked across the paddock to Byron Creek. The sun was shining on his face and he slowly drifted off to sleep. Neil and Miles brought out mugs of milky tea and servings of sponge cake with jam and cream. Their father signalled for quiet with an index finger to his lips, while pointing to Andrew sleeping. No one spoke, but the family sat together in a companionable silence.

Andrew woke with a shiver an hour later when a cloud blocked the warm afternoon sun. He was surprised to find he was on his own on the veranda. He stood, stretched and walked back into the house to find Kate in the bedroom closing her overnight bag.

'Are you OK to drive me back to Brisbane earlier than planned?' she asked softly.

Andrew nodded and scooped the car keys up off the dresser. He picked up Kate's bag and walked through to the front veranda. His brothers had already left, and his father was repairing broken wire on the front gate.

'Dad, I'm driving Kate back to Brisbane,' he called out.

'When will you be back?' he responded.

'Don't know, I'll call you later to let you know.'

'OK son, drive safely.'

Charles walked over to kiss Kate goodbye.

'Bye Kate, and thank you again for a lovely meal.'

Kate smiled and got into the car. She knew what she wanted to say to Andrew, and hoped she had the courage.

The car was ten kilometres out of Bangalow before Andrew broke the silence.

'That was a lovely meal Kate. Thank you.'

Kate nodded.

'I'm sorry. I know I've not been very communicative these last twenty-four hours,' Andrew continued. 'There's been a lot to take in.'

She nodded again then asked, 'So what's next?'

'I don't know,' he replied. 'I guess I'll drop you off and come back down to Dad's place.'

'I mean, are you, were you, the baby's father?'

Silence, and then Andrew replied softly, 'I don't know.'

'So, it's possible?' Kate asked.

'Yes.'

'I see,' was all she could think to say.

'It was before you Kate, before us,' Andrew continued.

'And how do you feel about her now?'

Andrew looked out the car window and said nothing for a moment.

'I feel so many things. I'm tired and I'm confused. And I'd be lying to you if I denied my feelings for her.'

'I see,' she said again. 'Thank you for your honesty. I've often entertained the possibility that I was *rebound girl*. It seems my suspicions were true.'

They both looked at the traffic in front of them and said nothing for a few minutes.

'So,' Kate finally announced, 'this is what we'll do. I'll let everyone know that we have delayed the wedding. And you'll sort out your feelings for her, and your feelings for me. I can't have part of you. I won't. It's not fair. It's all or nothing.'

'Of course. It's what you deserve,' Andrew replied.

Kate reached over and turned the radio on, signalling that no further words were needed. The silence hung heavily, but there was nothing more to say. Listening to the late afternoon presenter chat about the news head-lines made it feel like there was someone else with them in the car.

Andrew dropped Kate off outside Admiralty Towers in the city at five o'clock. He watched her walk into the apartment block and then looked up to the sky. The sun set, marking the end of a long day and possibly the end of a chapter in Andrew's life. He picked up his phone and called George.

'How is she now?'

'Sleeping. Always sleeping, and she's so restless when she sleeps. She woke briefly and I practically had to force feed her.' He paused. 'I'm worried, Andrew. Her body is battered as is her spirit. I don't think she wants to ...' he hesitated, 'to get better.'

Andrew reflected on what George wasn't saying.

'I'll be there soon. We can talk about how best to help her. There are counsellors at the hospital and Dad wants to help too, in fact all the Wyatts are here to support you and Melissa. Which reminds me – are you OK? Have you eaten? You need to look after yourself too.'

'I'm fine. Really, I'm fine. Helen is here with me. I'm not alone.'

'Good. Good. I'll be there around seven and we can have something to eat together.'

'Very well. Drive safely Andrew.'

Both men hung up feeling a little better. Andrew started mentally preparing a list of things to do. He decided to call in at Melissa's house at Currumbin on the way down. Whoever Ben was to Melissa, he'd need to know about the accident. He started the ignition, turned the car towards Ann Street then on to the Riverside Express, and headed south to Currumbin.

*A*ndrew knocked loudly on the door of Melissa's house. He could hear music inside so knew someone was home. The door opened and Ben looks bemused.

'Hello again. She's not here,' he started, 'she's spending the weekend ...'

'I know,' Andrew interrupted. 'There's been an accident Ben. It's Ben, isn't it? Can I come in?'

'Melissa?' Ben whispered.

'Yes,' Andrew replied

'Oh no.'

Ben momentarily closed his eyes and then opened the door completely, and then rushed inside to turn off the stereo. Andrew was standing at the back door when he returned.

'What's happened? How is she?' Ben spluttered.

'We don't know exactly what happened. It was the storm. Many cars were involved. She has been badly hurt and is lucky to be alive.'

'And the little boy?'

So, Ben knew about the baby, Andrew noted.

'He didn't make it. I'm sorry.'

Ben sat down on the sofa and looked at his hands. Andrew sat down alongside him.

'So, where is she? Can I visit her?' he asked.

'She's at Byron Central Hospital. She ...' Andrew hesitated, 'I don't know if she wants visitors. She's lost in her own world of grief, hardly communicating, barely functioning. I just don't know.'

Ben looked at Andrew, as if to verify that he was telling the truth.

'I'll let you know if the situation changes. Perhaps you could give me your number?'

Ben reached over to his jacket slung on the back of the next chair and pulled a business card out from an inside pocket.

'Here,' he said simply. 'We both work at Niche Design. I guess I should tell them about the accident. Is that OK?'

'Yes of course. Just the accident, nothing else at this stage. That's important. Leave it for her to share ... anything else.'

'Yes of course, he replied. 'And I imagine that Niche will want to send flowers to the hospital. How long do you think she'll be there?'

'Don't know. It will depend on the speed of her recovery.'

'Is there anything else I can do for her?'

Andrew hesitated for a moment.

'Yes, there is. I am going to deal with the insurance company about her claim. Do you know where she keeps her records?

'Come with me. Let's look in her desk drawers.'

Andrew was struck by the smell of fresh paint as he walked into the study. He noticed that the walls were blue, and he felt overwhelmed with sadness. This room was clearly in the process of being converted into a nursery.

'Here it is,' Ben said, after a minute of searching.

Andrew looked at the statement and nodded.

'Thanks. That's all I need to contact them. And I should probably pick up some clothes for her. Is that OK with you?'

'Of course, this way.' Ben led Andrew into Melissa's bedroom. 'I'll go get a suitcase from the garage,' he offered and left Andrew alone.

It felt odd and intimate being in Melissa's bedroom without her. He opened the top drawer of her dresser to reveal her lingerie. Feeling confronted he closed it and moved to the second drawer. T-shirts, sweaters and blue jeans were organised neatly in piles. It was less invasive here and he selected a number of items which he laid out on the bed. He opened her wardrobe and also pulled out a denim jacket, slippers and pair of sneakers. Socks were needed, so he opened the top drawer again selecting two pairs and a selection of knickers. Her midnight blue nightdress was in the corner of the drawer. He pulled it to his face to feel its softness and remembered vividly seeing it fall from Melissa's shoulders last November. A piece of paper, wrapped up in the nightie, fluttered to the ground. He reached down to retrieve it and immediately recognised his handwriting. It was the note he wrote her when he told her that he loved her. He put the note and the nightie back in the top drawer and closed it.

Ben returned and opened the suitcase on a chair. Andrew moved the clothing into the suitcase and carried the bag outside to put in the boot of his car.

'Thanks for your help. I'll call tomorrow to let you know about a possible visit.'

The two men shook hands and Andrew got into his car and pulled his phone from his jacket pocket. He dialled his father and reached his voice mail.

'Hi Dad, just checking in as promised. I'm at Currumbin, at Melissa's place. I've picked up the insurance documents and a few of her clothes. I'll take them to the hospital now. Probably won't be home till late. Don't wait up. We'll talk tomorrow.'

Andrew arrived back at Byron Central Hospital at

7:30pm. He found George sitting on a chair beside Melissa's bed, scribbling in a notebook. George looked up and noticed the small suitcase Andrew was carrying.

'I picked up a few of her clothes on the way down,' Andrew whispered so as not to wake Melissa.

George smiled, and made a dramatic gesture of striking something from a list in his notebook. The two men walked out of the ward and into the waiting room so they could talk more freely.

'Thank you. That means a lot. She'll only need a few things here and hopefully she'll be able to come home in a few days.'

'Have you spoken with her today?'

"Spoken? No. Communicated with her, well, perhaps just a little. She nodded when I asked if she was comfortable. That was it.'

Andrew worried about how Melissa was feeling. George looked at his watch.

'It's 7:45. If you want to speak with her you should go now as we have been asked to observe official visiting hours from 10:00am until 8:00pm, now that she is out of danger. So you only have 15 minutes.'

Andrew walked quietly back into Melissa's ward. She was still sleeping so he leant over and kissed her on the forehead.

'Perhaps we can talk tomorrow,' he whispered.

Melissa didn't move. Andrew stroked her hand and looked at her pale face. There was a spider's web of scratches on the left side and a bruise that looked like Saturn on her right. He placed the suitcase in the corner of the room and then reached into his pocket and pulled out the tiny blue bonnet. He carefully tucked it under the blankets next to her shoulder.

'I thought you'd like to have this,' he whispered.

He quietly tiptoed to the door. Melissa's eyes began to flutter, just as he was leaving the room.

Andrew found George in reception.

'Was she awake?' he asked Andrew.

He shook his head.

'Maybe tomorrow.'

They walk companionably to the cafeteria and shared a sandwich together. Neither was very hungry. Andrew mentioned that he had found details of Melissa's car insurance and would contact them tomorrow. He also outlined the different ways the Wyatt family wanted to help.

'That's wonderful. Thank you. And please thank your father for me. With those jobs being taken care of I can focus 100% on getting her better. Her body is still broken and will heal in time, but that is not what I'm worried about. It's her heart. It's so hard to recover from the loss of someone you love. I know this. I wonder if there will ever be a day when I don't think of Ellen. I still miss her. And you know this too, of course, it's only eight months since your mum died.'

Andrew acknowledged this and said nothing. Silence hung companionably between the two men.

'We'll make sure she gets the help she needs,' Andrew offered. 'If not from us, then hopefully from the counsellors here at the hospital. There will be a way to help her to deal with this awful loss.'

The two men stood and walked out into the chilly June night air. They said nothing on the drive back to Bangalow until Andrew dropped George at his front gate.

'Tomorrow morning at 9:30?'

George nodded.

'Thank you again son. Thank you again for everything.'

Andrew smiled and waited until he saw that George had made it up the driveway and onto the front veranda. George waved to him as he opened the front door. Andrew flashed his car lights, and pulled out on to the road.

His father was drinking tea and reading *The Northern Star* at the kitchen table when he finally got home.

'Cup of tea? Just made a fresh pot.'

'Thanks Dad.'

Andrew took off his jacket and sat down at the table while his father fetched another cup.

'How's George?' his father asked while filling his cup.

'He's holding up. He's very grateful for the offer of support with those jobs. That reminds me, I should contact the police about getting an accident report.'

Andrew typed a note to himself in his phone.

'And Melissa?'

'Hard to know. She wasn't awake. She's in the best place for now I suppose.' Andrew hesitated before continuing. 'We just don't know what's going on in her head.'

'And what about Kate?'

Andrew sighed.

'I don't know. I think I've blown it. For the moment we've agreed to delay the wedding. We'll see. I'll need to spend time with her. Can you tell the boys about the wedding?'

His father nodded.

'What are your plans for tomorrow?'

'I'll play it by ear. I'll take George to the hospital, visit the police and I promised to contact Ben.'

'Ben?' Charles queried. 'Who's he?'

'Ben is ...' Andrew hesitated. 'He works with Melissa.'

'I see,' his father replied simply. 'And don't you need to prepare for your Perth meetings next week?'

'Damn. I'd forgotten about the conference and those meetings. It's a busy agenda as I had cleared a week from the 24th for the wedding and honeymoon. I can't delegate or defer any of it. Damn.'

Andrew sighed and looked at the calendar on his phone.

'You'd better get to bed son. You've a busy day tomorrow and a full week ahead.'

Andrew nodded, collected the mugs and deposited them in the kitchen. In bed, as he pulled the blankets up close to his shoulders he thought of Melissa and wondered if she was awake.

JUNE 9 – LATE EVENING

*M*elissa listened to the sounds of retreating footsteps and opened her eyes. The room was dark, but a shaft of light from the corridor allowed her to see an outline of furniture. Her eyes scanned the room. There was a jug of water and plastic glass on her bedside table and she suddenly realised she was thirsty. She attempted to roll towards the table and felt an explosion of pain from the bruises along her body. Groaning, she rolled back onto her back. She felt an unfamiliar bundle under her shoulder. She carefully reached over her shoulder and tentatively pulled out what looked like a ball of wool in the darkness. She brought the wool to her face and when it caressed her cheek she instantly knew that this was the tiny hat from her son's head. Her body started convulsing as grief took hold. Her sobs attracted the attention of a nearby nurse.

'Are you OK Mrs Brinkley?' she asked quietly as she approached the bed.

'I'm thirsty,' Melissa replied, as she used the bonnet to wipe the tears from her eyes.

The nurse helped her to sit up in the bed and then poured her a glass of water. Her eyes examined Melissa's face as she passed her the glass.

'You've been through a lot. You should talk to someone.'

Melissa gulped down the water, and with a shaking hand, passed the empty glass back to the nurse. She slowly and painfully slipped down again beneath the blankets. The nurse checked the covers, watching her patient. She pulled the clipboard from the end of the bed to make a few notes. Melissa's eyes were closed again. The nurse doubted she was asleep but knew that this fragile patient was not yet ready to talk about her pain. With nothing more to be said she left.

The tiny bonnet was clasped tightly in Melissa's hands. She kissed it and breathed in the scent of her son, remembering how wonderful it felt to hold him in her arms. She wondered where they had placed his tiny body and became distressed imagining him alone in a room. Tears again overflowed and ran down her cheeks. Everything was gone – her son – the plans she had for their life. Everything. Melissa could see nothing ahead but emptiness. There was no future. And then she rationalised that she deserved this – that she had been punished for loving another man while married to Jonathan. Her mood darkened as she slipped into a deep and fitful sleep.

George was standing ready at his front gate when Andrew pulled in to collect him on Sunday morning. He was carrying a metal flask and a large plastic container.

'I don't think I can do another day of hospital coffee,' he offered with a smile. Andrew was pleased to see that George was able to joke. These last two days had been emotionally draining so it was good to have a little humour.

They passed the twenty-minute drive from Bangalow to Byron Bay in silence, listening to the radio. They pulled into a now familiar spot in the parking lot. As they entered the hospital they were greeted by Helen, who motioned them to three chairs in the corner. They sat down and looked at her, anxious for news.

'I think that you should wait here. I just passed Melissa's ward and saw that Doctor McDonald was with her.'

The men nodded and neither spoke, each lost in his own thoughts.

Helen looked at the plastic container and flask on the floor besides George.

'What's this?' she asked.

'Some decent coffee and a few leftover cakes.'

'Lovely,' she replied.

Doctor McDonald arrived in the waiting room and walked towards them. Helen stood, smiled and left. Andrew was touched by her grace and tact.

Doctor McDonald sat down in the seat vacated by Helen.

'How are you both today?' she asked.

Well, the news can't be too bad if she is asking about us, Andrew thought to himself.

'We're fine,' George replied. 'But how's Melissa?'

'She's awake now, but she's had an unsettled night.'

This news hung heavily.

'Can we see her?' George asked.

'Give us an hour or so. The nurses are going to wash her, either in bed or in the shower. This will not be a quick process. We'd like to see if we could get her out of bed. Then I want the hospital counsellor to see her and make an assessment. Grief is such a tricky thing, without the complications of physical injury. Let's talk again after I've spoken with the counsellor.'

Andrew and George nodded and the doctor left to complete her rounds. Andrew turned to Melissa's father.

'I think I'll go to the police station to get a copy of the accident report. I shouldn't be too long.'

'OK,' he replied simply. 'And thank you again for taking care of this.'

Andrew smiled, patted George on the shoulder and walked outside to his car.

It was a short drive to the police station. There were a number of tired looking locals in reception and Andrew had the impression the station had seen a busy night. He was given a copy of the accident report and directions to the car lot where Melissa's car had been stored. He was greeted by the barking of an enthusiastic Doberman, fully embracing his role as guard dog.

'Settle down Fred.' A call was heard from the back of the yard.

Andrew waved and the parking lot attendant unlocked the gate to the yard. He showed him the paperwork from the police station.

'Follow me, it's down the back.'

They wove their way through twenty cars, some impounded from overstaying time in a designated parking space and others as the result of an accident.

'That's it,' Andrew said simply, pointing to Melissa's car in the corner.

'Goodness me,' the attendant remarked thoughtlessly, 'did anyone make it out of that car alive?'

Andrew didn't respond. He took a photo of the car from the front and then walked around to the driver's side. The blood-splattered air bag hung lifelessly on the steering wheel. He took a deep breath and moved closer. Broken glass was sprinkled across the driver's seat and floor. He noticed Melissa's handbag and papers on the passenger side floor. He moved to the other side of the car, placed his jacket across the open window to protect himself from the broken glass and leaned in to retrieve her things. The back end of the car had damage consistent with another car slamming into it at full force. If there was anything in the boot, it would be beyond use now.

'To the scrap yard now?' the attendant asked.

'Probably,' Andrew responded. 'I'll call you later to confirm.'

Large raindrops from a darkening sky ended the conversation and Andrew ran to his car to escape the approaching storm.

Melissa watched the morning light arrive slowly and listened to the distant rumble of thunder. Weariness cloaked her but she was unable to sleep. She was still holding the blue bonnet against her cheek while listening to the whispers of nurses and the rattling of trolleys.

An orderly approached her bed and placed a breakfast tray on the pivoting table. Melissa viewed it without interest. As the orderly left, a nurse entered.

'Good morning,' she said with a perfunctory smile, while swinging the portable table with the breakfast tray closer to Melissa. 'Let me help you get comfortable so you can eat something.'

'I'm comfortable thank you. Perhaps later,' Melissa replied politely, without moving from her position. The nurse examined her face, paused for a moment and left.

Melissa listened to the thunder and felt anxious. In her exhaustion, she was transported back to Friday afternoon when she was rushing to get ahead of the storm and to the safety of her father's home. The details of the drive remained sketchy, no matter how hard she tried to recall them. The drive out of Byron Bay along Ewingsdale Road was a familiar one, but she could only recall old memories of uneventful journeys. A breakfast tray crashing to the floor brought back the sound of hail on the roof of the car. Moments later there was screaming, and someone was pulling at her hand. Melissa woke up with a start, realising she'd been screaming in her sleep, and her restless movements had knocked the breakfast tray to the floor. The orderly had come rushing back, followed by the nurse and Doctor McDonald. No-one spoke while the crockery was collected and the floor mopped. The doctor asked the orderly to fetch another breakfast tray, and then she and the nurse moved to opposite sides of the bed.

'Let's help you to get more comfortable,' the nurse proposed. The request didn't sound like a suggestion and Melissa reluctantly started to sit up with the help of the doctor and nurse, who placed additional pillows behind her back. Pain wracked her body and tears filled her eyes. The orderly returned and placed a new tray on the pivoting table.

'Milk?' the nurse asked while pouring Melissa a cup of tea. She nodded and held the warm mug with both hands trembling, lifting it gently to her lips. The warm brew was soothing and familiar.

'Thank you,' she said returning the mug to her tray.

'Good,' replied the nurse. 'Now eat some of your scrambled eggs and I'll be back in a bit to help you get ready for your shower.'

Again, the instructions were delivered without an option for refusal. Before Melissa could reply, the nurse had turned and moved on to her next patient. She reluctantly picked up her fork and ate the scrambled eggs as instructed. On finishing the meal, she pushed the tray away as far as possible to avoid further mishaps. Her eyes scanned the bed for the blue bonnet and she became agitated when she couldn't see it.

Doctor McDonald entered the room and noticed her distress.

'What's up Melissa?' she asked quietly.

'I can't find the bonnet. I can't have lost it. It was here. I had it before.'

The doctor put down her clipboard and motioned to the nurse attending another patient. They both checked the covers and the nurse quickly found the bonnet under one of the pillows. Melissa nodded in appreciation and held it against her cheek.

'One of the assistant nurses will be here shortly to help you to have a shower,' the doctor started, 'and then Connie from the hospital support team will call by to introduce herself.'

Melissa knew immediately that *the support team* was code for a counsellor.

'I don't think I'll be able to get out of bed to have a shower.'

'Yes, that's probably true. But we'll try.' The doctor paused before continuing. 'There will be pain, but you can't get to recovery until you go through the pain.'

Melissa sensed that the doctor was not just referring to the physical pain.

'If you can make it out of bed and wash, we can put you in some of your own clothes,' the doctor said pointing to a small suitcase in the corner. 'You'll feel more comfortable out of this designer hospital wear.' Melissa didn't respond to the doctor's joke and stared at the suitcase. She was sure she'd packed a different bag for her weekend with her father. A young assistant nurse arrived at the bed with a shower chair and the nurse who insisted she eat her scrambled eggs. The bossy nurse briskly pulled off her bedcovers, knocking the bonnet out of Melissa's hands. She grabbed it back and held it close to her chest. Sensing Melissa's distress, the doctor opened a drawer in the bedside cabinet.

'Let's put that bonnet in here for safe keeping while you have a shower and they change your sheets.' Melissa reluctantly passed the bonnet to the doctor and watched her place it gently inside the cabinet drawer. Knowing that this precious part of her son was safe she felt obliged to acquiesce to the doctor's demands. The assistant nurse pulled the covers all the way back from Melissa's legs. She shivered.

'Can you swing your legs off the bed?' the doctor asked.

She tried and was stabbed by acute pain in her abdomen. The nurse reached across and wrapped both legs in her arms, swinging them gently off the bed. Melissa closed her eyes and gritted her teeth as pain bounced around her body like a pinball. The pain subsided and she opened her eyes to see that she was flanked by a nurse on one side and the assistant nurse on the other.

'Ready,' the nurse called out, and before she had time to take in what was happening, Melissa was lifted into a shower chair. Pain again flared at multiple points in her body.

'Use the swing next time,' the nurse told the assistant before leaving.

The assistant nurse opened the small suitcase on the bed besides Melissa.

'Why don't you choose what you want to wear while I go and see if the bathroom is still free?'

Melissa lifted out a long-sleeved black t-shirt, track pants and knickers. She knew for sure she didn't pack these clothes and wondered who did. The nurse returned and wheeled her into the bathroom. She placed the fresh clothes on a rack and undid the ties down the back of the gown. The stiff cotton garment fell off her shoulders to her waist. Melissa turned her head to the right and gasped as she saw her reflection for the first time. There was a deep black shadow on one side of her face and a spider's web of scratches on the other. Matching bruises on her shoulders and ribs reminded her of the spots on a Dalmatian. It was surreal. She didn't recognise herself in the dark eyes staring back in the mirror. A blast of warm water on her back broke her stare and she closed her eyes to enjoy the feeling. The nurse expertly removed the gown while she remained seated in the shower chair and passed her the hand spray so she could continue washing herself. The assistant nurse tugged at the now damp bandages and peeled them away. A few minutes later all bandages have been removed, wounds inspected and new bandages applied. The incision from the caesarean section was attended to last. Melissa stared at the stiches marking her son's entry point into the world. Another moment she has missed in his tiny life. A new bandage covered the wound, and the long-sleeved t-shirt now covered the bandage. The assistant nurse helped her with her knickers and tracksuit pants and threw the towel in the basket.

'Phew. All done. Perhaps next time we could ask one of the volunteers to wash your hair.'

Melissa said nothing and was wheeled back to her bed. The assistant nurse placed a brace around her which was connected to a hoist. The straps rubbed on Melissa's bruises and she cried out in pain.

'OK then. You'll have to help me get you back into bed.'

Melissa nodded. The straps were removed and she followed directions to stand up and lean against the bed. She moved slowly to contain the pain. The bedcovers were pulled back and she turned and gently sat down. The assistant nurse moved her legs up and together they shuffled her back under the sheets. The pillows were puffed and placed behind her and the assistant nurse departed with the shower chair. She was exhausted and closed her eyes. Moments later she heard footsteps approaching the bed and opened her eyes again.

'Hello there,' said the woman with a broad smile. Melissa didn't recognise her but noticed the word *Coun-*

sellor on the badge on her lapel. 'My name is Connie and I work at the hospital,' she offered not waiting for a response.

'I see,' Melissa replied simply.

'Always available if you want someone to chat to,' Connie continued.

Melissa sighed and was about to respond when she heard a familiar voice from the doorway.

'You look awful Mel,' Ben proclaimed, striding over to the bed. He was holding a large bunch of lilies and had a shocked expression on his face.

'I'm fine thanks Connie,' Melissa said.

'OK then. I see you have company. Would you like for me to arrange to get those flowers in some water?'

'Yes, that would be great. Thank you.'

Ben passed the flowers to Connie and pulled a chair up close to the bed. He reached out and stroked Melissa's arm.

'I'm so sorry Mel,' he started, 'I can't imagine what you're going through.'

Melissa patted his hand. An awkward silence hung for a moment with neither sure of what to say next.

'Thank you for the flowers,' she offered. 'And I guess I need to thank you for bringing fresh clothes.'

'Nope. Wasn't me. That was your neighbour from Bangalow. The same guy who dropped off the fruit box.'

'Oh,' she spluttered, pausing before continuing. 'When did you see him?'

'Yesterday. He called by to let me know about the accident and to see if we could find the car insurance documents.'

Melissa stopped talking, momentarily lost in her thoughts.

Andrew saw George and Helen near the café as he entered the hospital. Heads close together, they looked like old friends as they illicitly shared cake from George's plastic container, hoping that they were not caught by the café owners. They looked up, smiling, as Andrew approached.

'How did you go?' George asked. Andrew gave the thumbs up sign. 'Got the accident report and supporting photos – and I retrieved Melissa's handbag and work documents.'

'Excellent. She will be pleased. Why don't you go and see her? She should be finished with the counsellor by now.'

Andrew could hear voices as he approached Melissa's ward and assumed that the counsellor must still be there. He tentatively looked around the door and found Ben sitting in a chair pulled up close to the bed. Unsure what to do, and wishing to avoid interrupting an intimate conversation, he waited outside. He could hear snatches of conversation about a fruit box and insurance documents so decided to go in.

'You were meant to call me,' Ben called out to Andrew as he looked up and saw him approaching the bed.

'I was, and I didn't and I'm sorry,' Andrew heard himself sprouting defensively.

A nurse hustled past him with a beautiful arrangement of lilies. Their scent masked the underlying perfume of hospital disinfectant. Andrew felt guilty at not having brought flowers himself.

'They're lovely,' he offered, noticing Ben's broad smile.

He was uncertain what to say next, still wondering if he had interrupted an intimate moment. He noticed that she was wearing the black t-shirt he'd packed for her.

'Umm, I'm just dropping off Melissa's handbag and folio. I pulled them from her car this morning.' Andrew was embarrassed that he had talked to Ben about Melissa in the third person, when she was lying there watching him. He made the decision to leave.

'I'll just leave it here for now. I have to go. I have to go back to Brisbane, and then I am away in Perth for the next ten days. Perhaps you could call me Melissa? When you feel up to it?' he said addressing her directly.

Melissa nodded and Andrew smiled. There was a connection. If only Ben wasn't there, he could talk to her, he could hold her. He looked into her eyes one last time and reluctantly left.

Melissa watched him go.

'Ten days,' she thought to herself. 'He'll be back in ten days, just before his wedding.'

Her thoughts were interrupted by Ben.

'Should I have left?' he asked.

'No, it's fine. Thank you for coming. I'm pleased to see you.'

They talked about work but Melissa was distracted. She needed to tell Andrew about the baby, about his son.

Andrew called into the cafeteria on his way out. Helen and George were still chatting. George looked up as he approached.

'That was quick?' George said with surprise.

'She has company,' he replied, 'and I need to get back to Brisbane – I'm flying out to Perth tomorrow morning.

'How long will you be gone?' George asked.

'Ten days.'

George hesitated before responding.

'You'll be back just in time for your wedding.'

'There's no wedding, well, at least – not for now.' Andrew hesitated before responding. 'It's complicated.'

George nodded. He had a fair idea of what the complication was.

'Should I call Dad to come and get you later – to take you home?

'No. I'm fine son,' he replied, looking at Helen. 'Drive safely and keep in touch. Please.'

'I will. I promise,' Andrew replied. He patted George on the shoulder and nodded at Helen before standing to leave. He hesitated as though he was about to say something else, but changed his mind, turned and left.

George rested his chin in the palm of his hands and looked at Helen.

'Those two. I just don't know what to do about them.'

'Go and see you daughter,' Helen offered. 'You'll know what to say and do when the time is right.'

George followed the orderly with the lunch tray into Melissa's ward. He saw the young man with the sandy hair and freckled complexion talking animatedly with Melissa.

'It's good to see you sitting up,' he said to announce his arrival.

He walked over and kissed his daughter on the forehead and then pushed the pivoting table with lunch in front of her.

'Eat,' he said simply.

Melissa knew that this was not a request.

Ben stood to leave.

'I'll be off then.'

'Dad, this is Ben, my lodger.'

George shook his hand.

'I'll call you Tuesday arvo to let you know about work stuff. Mel, do you have a phone?'

'Can you look in my handbag Ben?'

He fumbled around inside and retrieved her phone. He tried to turn it on without success.

'Needs charging,' he offered. He pulled a charger from her bag and plugged one end into the phone and the other into a socket in the corner of the room. The phone beeped and a light appeared on the screen.

'You should know in an hour if it's OK.'

Ben walked around to the other side of the bed. He patted her hand, kissed her on the forehead and gave a final wave as he walked out the door.

'Eat, please,' her father instructed, a little more firmly this time.

While Melissa picked up her cutlery and took a mouthful of pasta, George scooped up the handbag and folio and put them in the bedside cabinet drawer. He noticed the blue bonnet inside and suddenly felt sad. Melissa looked at her father looking at the bonnet.

'Can you pass that here, Dad,' she whispered.

George lifted the tiny bonnet out and passed it to his daughter. They both started crying. Melissa held the bonnet in her left hand and her father's hand in her right. He put his head on her mattress and closed his eyes. He felt tired, sad and frustrated. If only Andrew and Melissa had shared their grief. He was certain she hadn't told him that he was the father. Several minutes passed before he lifted his head to look at his daughter. She had fallen asleep, clutching the baby's bonnet. He quietly pushed the food table away and pulled the blankets up over his daughter. He kissed her and tiptoed out of the ward. He walked past the cafeteria and reception and out into the winter sunshine. He needed a stroll to clear the cobwebs.

Twenty minutes later, Helen passed by Melissa's ward. She could see that she was stirring so walked over to her bed pulling her trolley behind her.

'Would you like a cup of tea dear?' Helen asked softly.

'Who are you?' Melissa asked suspiciously, thinking the 'tea lady' was a counsellor in disguise.

'I'm Helen.'

'And what do you do?'

'I pour cups of tea,' Helen replied with a wide smile. 'May I?' she added.

Melissa nodded and Helen poured tea into a large mug. She also reached into her trolley and pulled out a plate of sandwiches.

'Thank you,' Melissa replied, feeling embarrassed at her defensiveness. She was still clutching the blue bonnet.

'What's your son's name?' Helen asked.

'Scott,' Melissa replied without hesitation.

'That's my favourite name in the world,' Helen replied. 'My grandson is called Scott. He's four years old, going on ten. Very inquisitive and full of life.'

'My son only lived a day.'

'Oh. That would be a day in our world, but not a day in yours. I imagine Scott has been a part of your life and for many months now,' Helen replied.

Melissa nodded as a tear ran down her cheek. She remembered the kicks and the rolls and the whispered conversations late at night. There were plans for a future they were going to share together.

'You're awake?'

Melissa looked up to see her father approaching the bed. George saw there had been tears and that now there was tea and sandwiches on the tray.

'I'll leave you with your Dad,' Helen said quietly before leaving.

'What a lovely lady,' Melissa whispered, watching her walk across the ward to another patient.

'I think so too,' George said, a curious smile on his face. 'Eat a sandwich love. You'll feel better.'

Melissa sipped her tea and ate a chicken sandwich. Her father scanned the front page of *The Northern Star* which he'd collected on his walk. He looked up to see Melissa looking at him.

'Yes?' he enquired. 'Something you want to tell me?

'Your grandson's name is Scott.'

'That's lovely darling. Just lovely. Did you tell Andrew?'

'I didn't get a chance Dad. To tell him anything.'

'You know he cares about you a great deal.'

'I know. I can see that. But I don't want to complicate his life. He's getting married in two weeks.'

'I'm not sure the wedding is happening now.'

Melissa took in the news.

'Dad, can you pass me my phone?' George retrieved the phone and passed it to her. She tried without success to make a call. 'I think it's been damaged in the crash. Do you have your phone on you?'

'Sorry love – forgot it. Tomorrow, I'll bring it without fail. I promise. Let me take your phone and I'll see what I can do. It'll probably have to wait 'til Tuesday now. None of the shops are open over the long weekend.'

Melissa had lost track of time. It was only Sunday. Two days since the accident. How the world had changed. She felt tired.

'I'm just going to have a nap.'

'That's OK dear. You go to sleep,' he replied. 'I'm just going to sit here reading the paper.'

Melissa closed her eyes and drifted off into a deep sleep.

At 5:00pm the doctor called by on her rounds.

'I'm pleased she's sleeping. How is she?'

'Better,' George said. 'She's eaten a little and told me the name of my grandson. So ... small steps.'

'Good – pleased to hear it. And she made it out of bed

to shower this morning – well, with assistance. This is good too. I'll push her tomorrow to walk. I can't release her into your care until she can make it to the bathroom on her own.'

'Well, that's a source of motivation if I've ever heard one,' George offered.

'A meal here?' the orderly asked.

Doctor McDonald and George both looked at Melissa deep in sleep.

'No, not this evening,' Doctor McDonald replied. 'I think sleep is more important than food for now.'

George nodded in agreement as he sat down and picked up the paper. He fell asleep in the chair and was woken by Helen an hour later.

'Ready to go?' she asked.

He smiled, stood up, kissed his daughter again. They then walked out of the hospital together.

JUNE 11 – BYRON BAY

*M*elissa could smell the scent of lilies before she opened her eyes. In the darkness of the early morning she was initially disoriented. The sound of hushed whispers and slow-moving trolleys reminded her that she was still in hospital. She needed to visit the bathroom so pressed the button beside the bed and an assistant nurse came to help her into the wheelchair. She was still stiff and sore but the process of getting in and out of bed was a little easier today. As she was settling back into bed the orderly brought in breakfast. She ate it all without resistance.

The doctor called by at 7:15am and was delighted with her for having finished breakfast and made it to the bathroom.

'Excellent progress Melissa. If you're up for it, I'll get your Dad to take you for a spin later.'

Melissa nodded. The doctor continued with her rounds and Melissa searched for the baby bonnet. She clasped this precious item close to her chest and settled back down into the covers.

Her father arrived with Helen at precisely 10:00am.

'Hello Dad, Helen,' she said glancing between them.

'Helen is my designated driver today,' her father offered unprompted.

Melissa smiled.

'How you feeling, love?'

'More myself. I slept well and long.'

'Yes, a real sleeping beauty,' piped the doctor, who had just returned with a nurse and a wheelchair. 'It's a lovely day outside, let's get you some fresh air.'

The nurse helped Melissa out of bed and wrapped her legs and shoulders with a blanket.

'The bonnet,' Melissa said to her father. He picked up the bonnet off the bed and with his daughter's nod of approval, placed it in the first drawer of her cabinet. Satisfied that Scott's bonnet was safe, she motioned to her father to let him know she was OK to go outside.

The cool winter air shocked her senses, but she was delighted by the fresh air. They stopped at a bench where her father engaged the brake and pulled a flask of coffee from inside his jacket pocket.

'The hospital coffee here does not improve with familiarity.'

Melissa smiled at her father.

They sat companionable for a few minutes saying nothing.

'So, what's next?' George asked softly.

'I'm torn between going back to work as soon as I can and running away.'

'Ah, yes running away.' George offered thoughtfully. 'The trouble with this option is that you can't run away from your grief. It travels with you. Believe me, changing locations does not change your pain. Honey, you've lost a child, you've lost your son ... and all the hopes and plans that went with him.' George paused before continuing. 'You're unlikely to ever get over it. You'll just get better at managing the hole.'

Melissa knew her father was describing the pain of losing her mother. She looked at her hands because it was too difficult to look at him.

'As soon as the doctor has cleared you to come home, *with me,*' he said, with emphasis, 'our first stop will be at the courthouse to register Scott's life and death. He was here, and he was real. And his life needs to be recognised.'

Melissa started sobbing and her father placed his arm around her shoulders, while reaching for a handkerchief from his pocket.

'We'll take it one step at a time. And I'll be here with you – for each step. And you should let Andrew support you as well. He's lost a son too. And he needs to know this.'

Melissa wiped the tears from her eyes with her father's hankie.

'Are you up to speaking with him yet?

'No,' she responded simply. 'But I'll try.'

George passed Melissa his phone.

'I'll give you some privacy. Take as long as you need.'

Melissa looked at the phone and then watched her father walk away. She couldn't remember Andrew's number but a search revealed her father had saved it as a favourite. This closeness between them was unexpected. After three rings she heard Andrew's voicemail instructing her to leave a message. She hung up immediately, unsure of what to say. Cradling the phone in her hands she ran through the possible messages she could leave. None of them felt right and leaving a message felt disrespectful, both to Andrew and to Scott. She resolved to speak to him in person, as soon as he was back. He deserved that.

Footsteps on the grass alerted her to her father's return.

'Voicemail,' she said simply.

'Ah yes, he's probably on his way to Perth.' He sat down again on the bench and looked into the distance.

'Honey,' he said after a few minutes have passed, 'you'll need to think about a funeral.'

'Ahh Dad. It's too soon. I can't. Most people don't even know I was pregnant.' Tears filled Melissa's eyes.

'The funeral is not for them, it's for you and it's for Scott.'

She didn't say anything and looked at her hands. Her father continued. 'We'll keep it small and private and we'll wait until Andrew is back next week.'

Melissa nodded.

'He said he's away for ten days and I'm fairly sure he's got next Friday off in preparation ...' George hesitated, 'for his wedding. We know he will most likely be free now.'

Melissa said nothing.

'I'll make enquiries for next Friday.'

George looked at his daughter.

'You're shivering. Let's get you back inside.'

The bossy nurse was in the ward when George wheeled Melissa back to her bed. She came over to assist with the lift from the wheelchair. Melissa squeaked in pain as she was lifted rather brusquely to a leaning position against the bed.

'Can you let go of the bed and stand on your own?' she asked Melissa.

'I don't think so.'

'Please try,' the nurse instructed in a tone that indicated that this was not a request.

Melissa slowly released her full weight back on to her feet.

'Argh,' Melissa cried out while leaning back against the bed.

'We'll try again tomorrow,' the nurse replied matter-of-factly.

She helped Melissa to get seated on the bed, lifting her legs and getting her settled under the covers.

'How are we today?' asked the counsellor who had joined a growing party at Melissa's bedside.

'I'm better thank you,' Melissa said more sternly than she expected. 'I have my family here and I'm fine, thank you.'

The counsellor nodded and left, hearing the unsaid message very clearly. The nurse followed her out.

'You were a bit abrupt,' her father whispered.

'I'm a bit overwhelmed Dad. I feel like I'm being forced to do and say things ... before I'm ready.'

'Honey, if you were to wait – well – you may never be ready. Don't you want to get out of here? You can't hide from the pain. Confront it and get on with your life.'

Now her father was being a bully. She looked at his

kind face and knew that his *bossiness* was coming from love.

'I'll try harder. I will.'

He patted her hand.

'I'll go buy the paper. Do you want anything?'

She shook her head and smiled. As her father left, the orderly arrived with her lunch tray. The tomato soup warmed her body and she snuggled down under the covers, letting sleep overwhelm her.

When she woke several hours later her father was in the chair reading the *Northern Star*.

'Hello there sleeping beauty.'

'Hey. Have you finished the crossword yet?'

Her father smiled. This was more like the old Melissa. 'Nearly. What's a ten-letter word for pushy ending in 't'.

'Persistent,' Melissa replied without hesitation.

They both laughed.

'What a lovely sight,' offered Helen, approaching the bed. 'Tea, Melissa?'

'Yes please, but first a favour. Can you help me get into the wheelchair so I can get to the bathroom without dragon lady's help?'

'Of course.'

Helen fetched the wheelchair while George removed the covers from her legs. Together, they helped Melissa into the chair. She bit her lips hard to avoid squeaking in pain. Helen wheeled her into the bathroom and Melissa groaned when she caught a glimpse of herself in the mirror.

'Let me wash your hair tomorrow. It's an important part of your recovery.'

Melissa smiled.

'Thank you Helen. Just what I need.'

George was on the phone when they arrived back. He said thank you quickly to whoever he is was speaking to, hung up and moved to the side of the chair.

'Ready?'

Melissa nodded and they all worked together to help her lean against the bed. She paused and then slowly let go to stand on her own, for just a moment. They all smiled and then helped her back under the covers.

Helen poured a cup of tea and placed it on the pivoting table.

'All is good for Friday week,' her father said.

Melissa looked at her father. 'Can you get me his bonnet Dad?'

George reached into the drawer and passed her Scott's bonnet.

She stroked her face with the tiny woollen bundle and then looked at Helen.

'We're going to celebrate Scott's life next Friday. Can you come?'

'Thank you. I'd love to be there,' Helen replied. She smiled and pushed the trolley to the next patient.

'I like her,' Melissa said.

'That's good. I do too.'

JUNE 11 – PERTH

*A*ndrew's flight arrived an hour late into Perth. On a positive front, the extra time in the air allowed him time to polish his speech for the conference. He dropped his bag at the Hyatt and went directly to the restaurant to join his colleagues who'd also flown in that day. They had arranged side meetings all week to optimise networking opportunities. He didn't look at his phone until 6:00pm when he was back in his hotel room. He noticed a missed call from George and immediately hit the redial button.

'Andrew,' George offered simply.

'Is Melissa OK?'

'Yes, she's better. Much better. Thank you Andrew.' 'Um,' George paused. 'We've arranged a funeral for the baby, for next Friday. Can you come?'

'Of course.'

'Bangalow Presbyterian at 3:00.'

'I'll be there. Thanks for letting me know.'

There was silence.

'His name was Scott,' George added.

'I like that name. Thank you again for inviting me.'

There was silence again. 'Anything else?' Andrew asked.

'Ah,' George cleared his throat, hesitating. 'We look forward to seeing you Andrew. Both of us.'

'Me too.'

'See you Friday week.'

'Righto.'

They both hung up.

Andrew opened his phone and replayed the video from the hospital of the night the baby died. It was beautiful and intensely sad. He took a deep breath and called Melissa's mobile. He knew immediately that he was being put through to voice mail but stayed on the line to listen to her voice. He hung up before he could leave a message. Collecting his thoughts, he dialled again. After the beep he spoke.

'Melissa it's Andrew. Just spoke to your Dad. I'll be there next Friday ... for you. I hope you're ... you're feeling stronger.'

He hesitated. 'I've a photo and a video of your ... of your Scott that I will send through. I know that Friday will be incredibly difficult. I'm pleased that I can be there for you. That's it for now. Speak soon.'

He rang off and sent the photo and video through. It'd been a long day. He put his phone back in his pocket, and left for a walk to clear his head.

Tomorrow, maybe tomorrow, we'll speak.

JUNE 12

*A*ndrew woke early and checked his phone before getting out of bed. No messages. Disappointed, he showered and dressed. He took a taxi to the convention centre and joined his colleagues at the Liberty Café for a pre-conference briefing. He soon became caught up in meetings, presentations and panel discussions.

Melissa also woke early. Determined to get out of hospital as soon as she could, she flexed and released her leg muscles under the blankets, breathing deeply through the pain of each extension. The orderly arrived with her breakfast and she ate it all. Pushing the tray away she gently pulled her legs out from under the covers and sat on the side of the bed.

'Bravo,' said a friendly voice.

Melissa smiled at the assistant nurse approaching the bed.

'Can you help me get to the bathroom?'

'On foot?'

Melissa shrugged her shoulders, suddenly doubting her new-found resolve.

She leaned on the nurse, tentatively took a first step and screeched in pain. The pain subsided and she attempted another step. Shooting pain returned. She shook her head in defeat and was helped into the wheelchair.

'I bet you'll be able to make it tomorrow,' the assistant nurse offered cheerily, wheeling her into the bathroom.

George and Charles arrived shortly after ten. Andrew's father was carrying a dozen iceberg roses.

'Your father said that you were feeling better and wouldn't mind a visitor.'

Melissa smiled.

'Mum's favourite roses. How thoughtful. Thank you Charles.'

'I brought them for both of you,' he said, looking at George.

'You'll have to tell me what you've been sprinkling into your soil, mate, to achieve such a fragrant bloom,' George said with a mischievous tone.

Charles smiled and passed the flowers to the assistant nurse who left to find a vase. Andrew's father looked at Melissa.

'I'm sorry love. We're all so sorry about the accident. I have no words...' his voice trailed off.

'Here we go, this is all I could find,' the assistant nurse chirped having returned with the flowers in a jug.

'I'll be off then,' Charles announced.

'Thanks for the lift. I'll be in touch.'

Helen arrived at 11:00 with a smile and basket of toiletries.

'Ready?' she asked Melissa.

Melissa dramatically threw off the blankets and wiggled her legs to the side of the bed.

'Ready,' she replied.

George and Helen helped her into the shower chair and placed the basket on her lap.

The warm water felt wonderful, as did Helen's fingers as she massaged the shampoo into her hair. Twenty minutes later, Helen wheeled Melissa back to the ward. Her father was in his chair reading the paper.

'How was that?' he asked.

'Wonderful. Thank you Helen,' Melissa said smiling.

'Why don't you two go outside into the sunshine

while I pop into town to see if they've been able to fix your phone?'

'Good idea. And thank you again Helen, for everything.' Melissa offered effusively.

George put a blanket on her lap and shoulders and pushed his daughter outside into the winter sunshine. Melissa closed her eyes and inhaled the country air. She listened to the sounds of cows mooing in the distance and felt calm.

'I spoke to Andrew last night,' her father said suddenly.

Melissa snapped out of her reverie and looked at her father.

'I told him you were feeling better and that there would be a funeral ... next Friday.'

'And ...' she whispered.

'And I told him that you had named your son Scott.'

'And that was it?'

Her father nodded. 'It wasn't my place to say anything else.'

'Thanks Dad.'

He patted his daughter on the knee and opened his newspaper.

At one o'clock, he looked up from his paper to see Helen approaching.

'I've been asked to shoo you both inside so the patient can have some lunch,' she announced.

George looked at his watch. 'Goodness, look at the time.'

'I'm a bit hungry too, now I think about it,' Melissa said.

'For you,' Helen said simply passing the phone to her.

The small screen was illuminated, revealing thirty emails, three messages and two missed calls.

'Let's get you back inside,' her father said turning the wheelchair around.

Melissa waited until she was settled under the covers before turning her attention again to the phone.

Message one: 'Jim here Melissa. Just wanted to say thanks again for all your work. Really thrilled with what you've proposed for the building. Excited to get moving. Give me a call next week and have a lovely weekend.'

Message two: 'Hi there. It's Dad. Bit worried about you, what with the wet and the traffic. We're coming down to ... to The Bay. Just call me when you get this. Love you.'

Message three: 'Melissa it's Andrew. Just spoke to your Dad. I'll be there next Friday ... for you. I hope you're ... you're feeling stronger ... I've a photo and a video of your ... of your Scott that I will send through. I know that Friday will be incredibly diffi-

cult. I'm pleased that I can be there ... for you. That's it for now. Speak soon.'

Melissa searched her emails for one from Andrew. There was no message in the email but two attachments. The first was a photo in a room she didn't recognise. There was a humidicrib with a small bundle wrapped in a white blanket with a clearly identifiable blue bonnet. It was difficult to see Scott's face, but two tiny clenched fists were visible from within the white blanket. He's so alone, Melissa thought to herself. She pressed the play button on the second attachment. Her father was holding Scott. She smiled. There was love in his eyes as he looked at his grandson before passing Scott over to her. She remembered the feel of his body and the smell of his head. She was cradling him as the video ended.

'Are you alright love?' her father asked softly.

Melissa hit the replay button and passed him the phone. Heads together, Helen and George watched the video in silence.

'So beautiful,' Helen said softly as George passed the phone back to his daughter.

'We're going for lunch in the café,' her father explained. 'Probably be about thirty minutes.' She smiled, knowing that her father was giving her time to call Andrew.

The phone rang twice before transferring to Andrew's voice mail.

'Oh Andrew. It's me. Melissa. I've only just got my phone back. It was broken in the accident and needed to be taken ... umm ...' She realised that she was beginning to babble. 'Anyway, I just, I just wanted to ring you and say thank you.'

She paused. 'The video is just lovely. There are no words that seem right ... I ... I feel ... it's the only photo I have of him.' Melissa started crying. 'So, thank you again.'

She ended the call and put the phone down. Moments later the phone rang.

'Andrew?' she answered quickly without looking at the screen.

'No, it's Ben. How are you Mel?'

'Better. Much better. Thank you. I'm hoping to be released tomorrow so that I can go to Dad's. All depends on what the doctor says.'

'Good. That's good. I spoke to Karen and told her about the accident. Just the accident. She told me to tell you not to worry about work, and to contact her when you felt up to it.'

'Thanks. I'll do that.' Melissa hesitated before continuing. 'Ben, I just wanted to let you know that we've arranged a funeral, Friday week, for Scott. It will be small, and I know it's a work day, but if you're able to come down to Bangalow ...'

'I'll be there Mel,' Ben said without hesitation.

'You've not eaten your lunch?'

Melissa looked up from the phone to see the doctor scrutinising her.

'I'm sorry, we were outside and lost track of the time.'

'Walking outside?' the doctor asked.

'No, not yet,' Melissa responded despondently.

'How mobile are you?'

Feeling a little defiant, Melissa pulled the bedcovers off and slipped her feet down to the floor. She held the bed covers and took a tentative and painful step on her own.

'Good,' said the doctor.

'A few more steps like that and a few more meals finished,' she said looking at the lunch tray, 'and I'll be happy to release you into suitable care. I assume that you're going to be looked after by your father.'

'Yes,' chimed in Helen who had just returned from the café with George, 'and by me. I'll be there to help.'

'Good,' said the doctor again, scribbling a note on her clipboard before leaving.

Helen helped Melissa back into bed and pulled the covers up. She then pushed Melissa's lunch tray in front of her. Melissa looked up smiling and made a dramatic gesture of picking up her fork. George smiled then sat back in his chair and opened the *Northern Star*. The afternoon passed quietly and George left with Helen at five o'clock so they could tidy the house in preparation for her arrival. Melissa watched the evening news to fill the hours until she fell asleep and inadvertently missed a call from Andrew. The phone was now in her bedside drawer next to the blue bonnet.

Andrew got back to his hotel room in Perth at 7pm. It was now nine in Byron Bay, so too late to call. He'd listened and re-listened to her message. He could hear her tears and was pleased that she sounded less helpless. Looking at his diary he felt frustrated at the distance between them.

𝓜elissa woke up early the next morning and carefully slid out of bed. She used the wheelchair as a walking frame and made it to the bathroom unassisted. She felt as if she'd climbed Everest. Her breakfast tray arrived as she returned and she made sure her plate was clean before the doctor arrived for her morning rounds. Alone in the ward, she watched the video of Scott again. She stroked her scar and sank into sadness. Sadness from the lost life: the cruel way he was snatched from her body when she wasn't awake; lost parenting stories with her father late into the evening over cups of tea; and major moments in Scott's undoubtedly bumpy journey to adulthood. She was going to be a parent and now she was just a widow.

'What are you watching love?' her father asked, interrupting her thoughts. She said nothing and passed him the phone. George watched the short video of Scott's last moments again and turned to Melissa.

'We have this. We're so lucky to have this. It's not much. But it's him. It's Scott. It's your son and my grandson … and it's,' George hesitated reaching for his handkerchief. He wiped his eyes. 'Can you send this to me?'

At that moment, it was clear to Melissa that she was not the only one who had suffered a loss.

'Is all OK here?' Doctor McDonald asked.

Melissa nodded.

'So how are you feeling today?'

'Sad,' was all Melissa could think to say.

'Well,' she paused, 'it's going to take a long time for the sadness to heal. Much, much longer than it will take for those bruises to disappear and for us to be able to look at your face without thinking we're peering through a spider's web.'

Melissa smiled at the doctor's uncanny humour and started crying. Her father passed her his handkerchief.

'So, Melissa, I understand you want to go home.' She looked at her clipboard and then back at her. 'You'll be staying with your father for a while?' Melissa nodded. 'And there will be someone to help you get in and out of the shower.'

'Yes,' replied George.

'And you'll take this card with the counsellor's

number on it, and you'll call her when you sink ... into sadness, which you will inevitably do.'

Melissa reached for the card. 'If I need to, I'll call, I promise.'

The doctor nodded and reached out to shake her and her father's hand.

'I wish you *both* the best for your recovery.'

'Righto,' George said with a forced cheeriness. 'You get your things together and I'll go and see where Miles has parked the car?'

'Miles?' Melissa queried.

"Yep. He's our designated driver today. Not only checking the cattle but driving the Cadillac.' George snickered at his play on words, while Melissa pulled the curtain round the bed to get dressed.

Melissa felt a sense of relief when Miles manoeuvred the car up the driveway. It was so good to be back in Banga-low. Miles carried Melissa's suitcase and handbag into the house, while her father held her arm, walking very slowly. Miles bounced down the steps to take her other arm.

'Cup of tea Miles?' George asked.

'Nope, I'm right thanks. I'll leave you to it. Should be back on Saturday with the new car. Andrew's got the paperwork all sorted.'

'That's great. Thanks. And please thank Andrew. Not that Melissa will be driving for a long while,' George replied, looking sternly at his daughter.

Melissa enjoyed watching her father in the kitchen warming up the casserole he had prepared the day before. Having a role as carer had given him focus and he regularly returned to his notepad to jot down new activities.

'After lunch I would strongly suggest you nap. Helen will be here later for your shower and we can all enjoy a light supper on the veranda.'

Melissa smiled.

'That plan is agreeable. Thank you Dad.'

She struggled as she stood.

'What are you doing dear?'

Melissa hobbled into the kitchen and put her arms around her surprised father.

'Thank you Dad. For everything. I'm very lucky to have you looking after me.'

❦

After a hearty lunch Melissa lay down on her childhood bed. She carefully placed Scott's bonnet under the covers and thought about how she would love to have shown him her room and to have taken him hunting for tadpoles. Her dad would have shown him how to mend a fence and help a cow struggling to deliver her calf. They would have climbed Mount Warning and run along Wategos beach. She imagined that she could hear his squeals of delight at digging for pipis and running from the waves continually reaching out to the ocean shore. It felt so real that she was sure she could hear him calling. She struggled in the bedclothes and walked towards the voices.

'She walks?' she heard. 'The mermaid walks.'

'Scott, that's a bit rude.'

In the shadows, Melissa made out the silhouette of a little boy.

'Scott,' she called out.

'You OK darling?' It was her father's voice.

Someone was holding her arm and she found herself staring at a little boy. He smiled at her. His blonde hair was familiar.

'It's you,' she whispered. 'Hello again.'

'You've met before?' her father enquired.

'At the beach. We met at Clarkes Beach. How are you Scott?'

Scott smiled.

'Good. I'm good,' he replied confidently. 'And I can't wait to tell Mason that I met the mermaid again,' he enthused before running outside.

George Bourne was confused and shook his head. 'Cup of tea for you on the veranda, when you're ready love.'

Melissa walked slowly to the bathroom, washed her

face and brushed her hair, rituals from a familiar routine. She was relieved to be out of hospital and almost back to normal life.

Scott was sitting on Helen's lap when Melissa walked on to the veranda.

'I hear you've met my grandson already?' Helen said with a smile.

'Yes, we're both water explorers.'

Scott giggled and George passed Melissa a cup of tea.

'Well I'm sure we can fit some underwater exploration into our Wednesday schedule,' Helen explained. 'Scott's with me each Wednesday after pre-school.'

'That would be lovely. I would really, really like that,' Melissa said softly, 'if that would be OK with Scott?

Scott nodded and slipped off his grandmother's lap, picking up several books on the floor before walking cautiously towards Melissa.

'Please could you read to me?' Scott suggested, passing her the books.

Melissa smiled and glanced down. Scott had given her *Finding Nemo* and *The Little Mermaid*.

'Of course,' she said, resisting the urge to stroke his hair.

'Why are you sad?' Scott asked.

'I … I knew another little boy called Scott,' Melissa stumbled on her words. 'And I miss him,' she said, tears rolling down her cheeks.

'Maybe he'll come back?' Scott offered helpfully.

Melissa shook her head.

'Sorry,' he said simply.

'Thank you.' Melissa reached out and stroked his hair.

'Can you read to me now,' he said attempting to climb onto her lap.

Melissa grimaced at the tugs to her stitches.

'Maybe next week Scott,' Helen said moving quickly towards them. 'Melissa is a bit sore today.'

'It's OK, Helen ... can you help?'

Helen lifted Scott as gently as she could onto Melissa's lap. There was pain, but she didn't care.

She sniffed his hair and put her arms around him to open the first page. Doctor McDonald's words suddenly come back to her, *there is recovery on the other side of pain*.

By Monday morning Melissa was quite mobile, cooking meals and washing clothes. This was important as she had so few clothes with her. She wanted to go back to Currumbin, but her father was insistent that she stayed. He liked having her there and was worried about her driving again so soon after the accident. Miles Wyatt had delivered her new car on Saturday and it had sat in the driveway tempting her. With a well laid out case made for collecting clothes and her laptop, together with a promise that she would return Wednesday, her father reluctantly agreed to let her go.

It was good to be behind the wheel again, although it was difficult. Melissa felt a little nervous, watching other drivers carefully and looking out for any unexpected activities. As she entered her driveway, she mentally congratulated herself on a milestone achieved. *One step, one day at a time.*

Her next milestone came sooner than expected when she walked into the study to see the freshly painted light blue walls. All the memories she had hoped to create in this room would now never be realised; it would always be a study. She picked up the laptop and walked out to the kitchen. This would now be her place of work.

There were over a hundred emails to be read and responded to. Melissa was touched to receive a note from the head of Niche Design asking her how she was feeling and requesting an informal catch-up – but only when she felt up to it. Melissa responded immediately, asking her if she would be open to coming to the house, as she was not yet ready to come into the office. Karen Knight responded within minutes saying that she would be available to come the following morning. Melissa was both pleased and a little nervous at her boss' enthusiasm for meeting with her. She wondered if there was a problem with her contract as she'd been off work for a week. She shrugged her shoulders. Losing a job would be easier than losing a son.

Ben arrived home at six and gave her a bear hug that took her breath away. It was nice to see him and they spent the evening talking about work. It was good to talk about things other than the accident. Ben insisted on cooking and washing up and Melissa found herself being sent to bed at eight o'clock.

'You know I came back to Currumbin to avoid being bossed around?' she tried to say with a stern face, but couldn't help smiling.

⸎

Karen Knight arrived at 11:00 the following morning with a basket of flowers.

'We rang the hospital and they said you'd gone to your Dad's place and couldn't give us the address. So, here they are – a bit late – but delivered with lots of good wishes – not just from me but from *everyone* at the office.'

'They're lovely. Really lovely Karen. Thank you.'

'New car?' Karen asked, more from a desire to keep the discussion light than from an interest in motor vehicles.

'Yes, from the insurance.'

'Ahh. Of course. Are you OK now?' she asked hesitatingly.

'I'm getting better, as they say, just taking it one day at a time. I should be able to come back to work soon.'

'Well, that's actually what I wanted to talk to you about.'

Melissa caught her breath and gestured for Karen to sit on the sofa.

'As you know, you were brought in to cover a period of maternity leave. Jane, she's the one who's had the baby, called me Friday to say that she didn't want to come back.

She was loving being at home with her son, and didn't want to miss a moment of his life. So, her job's available – if you want it.'

Melissa was stunned. She had been bracing herself for news that she was going to lose her job, and now she was being offered a permanent position. And the reason was because his mother *didn't want to miss a moment of his life.* Tears streamed down Melissa's face and Karen was both embarrassed and confused. She reached into her handbag for a packet of tissues and passed them to Melissa.

'I'm sorry. Let me explain. I didn't just lose a car in the accident. I lost my son,' Melissa whispered.

Karen inhaled in shock.

'I was a little over seven months pregnant.' Melissa continued. 'He was, we both were ... hurt in the accident. They delivered him by caesarean section, and he did his best to live. But it was too hard for him. It was too early. He had respiratory difficulties. He hung on for a day.'

'Oh. That's awful.' Karen gasped.

She took a tissue from the packet, wiped her eyes and moved closer to Melissa to put her arm around her. They sat in silence. Melissa reached into her handbag and pulled out the phone. She pressed *play* and passed the phone to Karen.

'This is my son ... Scott.'

Karen watched the video.

'That's lovely. Just lovely. Store this somewhere safe. It'll be an important memory.'

Melissa stared mesmerised at the final image of Scott.

'Oh Melissa,' Karen started, 'you have such a difficult journey ahead of you. Can I share with you something from my experience?'

Karen looked at Melissa.

'I miscarried at four months. I received a lot of support, but some people told me that I would get over it, and that I should get on with life, and have another baby.' She sighed. 'Well I tried. And indeed, I did fall pregnant twelve months later. But I'd lost a baby that was very wanted. And I still think of my little girl. Don't try to get over Scott – because you won't. Take the time to mourn him and don't hesitate to reach out to others who understand your loss.'

Melissa placed her hand on Karen's knee.

'Thank you for telling me about your little girl. It means a lot.'

Karen smiled and picked up her handbag. 'I'll be off then.'

They walked to the front door together.

'I hope that you'll include me in the list of people to whom you can reach out to – at any time.'

'I will, and thank you Karen ... for everything. And I'll let you know about the job very soon.'

*M*elissa lay in bed on Wednesday morning listening to a noisy chorus of rosellas in the tree beside her window. Her phone rang.

'Hey Dad,' she said swinging her legs out of bed.

'Hello darling. How are you today?'

'I'm,' she hesitated, 'I'm OK ... getting used to normal life again, bit by bit.'

'Good. Bit by bit. That's all you can hope for. It'll take time.'

'You're still coming down to The Bay today?'

'You bet. Looking forward to seeing you.'

'I realised this morning that we had forgotten to go to the court house. Let's do that today. It's time. Let's get an official record of Scott's life and we can talk about what needs to be said at his funeral.'

'Yes. Let's do that. Thanks Dad. See you at the court-house at 2:30?'

'Righto. And then we can meet Helen and the boys at the beach.'

Her father was sitting on a grey bench at the front of the courthouse as she parked her car on Middleton Street. He waved and they walked inside together. He looked over her shoulder as she handed in the birth registration statement and certificates.

'I like your son's second name,' he said and kissed her on the forehead.

Helen was sitting on a folding chair about thirty metres from the water's edge at Clarkes Beach. Scott and his friend were alternating between building sandcastles and racing each other along the shoreline. George opened another chair beside Helen, while Melissa walked down to join the boys. She loved the crunch of wet sand under her feet and took a deep breath to inhale the salty sea air. Two seagulls squabbling above pulled her eyes upward where she admired white fairy floss-like clouds drifting slowly across the sky.

'You were right, Scott,' came a shout from the shore-line. 'That's her. That's the mermaid.'

Scott smiled when Melissa sat down on the sand beside them.

'It's Mason, isn't it?' Mason nodded sheepishly before returning to dig out the moat around the castle. All three worked studiously. Melissa gently lay flat on the sand burrowing tunnels into the moat.

'You're very good at this,' Mason declared with admiration.

'She's got experience I think,' Scott chimed in with authority.

Melissa looked at him with a quizzical expression.

'The other Scott. Did you help him build castles too?' he clarified.

Melissa shook her head.

'Well I guess you've just got natural talent,' he asserted.

'Where is Scott number two?' Mason asked Melissa.

'Away,' Scott replied before she could respond.

'Hmmm,' murmured Mason, 'You should take a photo of our castle for him.'

'Excellent idea,' she responded. 'Dad,' Melissa called out to her father, pretending to take a photo with her hands.

George and Helen walked over and took a photo of the troupe.

'Good idea Mason. Thanks. And I'm going to write him a letter too.'

Melissa saw George and Helen furtively glance at each other.

'Let's run up the beach,' Mason yelled enthusiastically.

'Yeah,' screamed Scott, jumping to his feet.

'You know, swimming is more my thing than running,' Melissa said, rubbing her index finger on her chin, 'it's a mermaid thing.'

Scott and Mason looked at Melissa and then at each other.

'Go,' she shouted, and they raced off up the beach.

Melissa, George and Helen watched the boys run and soaked in their joy at this simple pleasure.

'So how are we going to get them back now George?' Helen asked leaning on his arm.

He grimaced and then yelled, 'Last one back to the car is a rotten egg.' The boys cried out and immediately changed running direction towards the car.

'An oldie but a goodie,' George said, pretending to polish his fingernails on his jacket. 'I haven't lost my touch.'

❦

Helen pressed the car door remote and called out to the boys to wipe their feet before getting in.

'Thanks for inviting me along, Helen. This was ...' Melissa struggled for words.

Helen hugged Melissa as a tear rolled down her cheek.

'The first of many seaside adventures, I'm sure,' Helen responded.

Melissa leant in the car window to say goodbye to Mason and Scott.

'That was fun.'

'You're crying?' Mason addressed to Melissa, a little confused.

'You know us mermaids. We leak from *everywhere*,' she said with emphasis, which caused both boys to giggle.

'See you next time.'

They waved goodbye.

After dinner that evening at her father's house, they discussed the order of service and Melissa wrote the eulogy. She passed the draft version to her father for comment. He put on his glasses and read it slowly.

'Perfect,' he said patting her hand. 'Will you be able to read it?

'I'll try.'

Helen arrived at the house for lunch on Thursday and brought with her framed photos of Scott taken at the hospital with Melissa and George. She had also had an order of service made including an image of the three of them.

'Oh Helen. These are lovely. So special. Thank you.'

'Was your father's idea,' Helen responded, 'I just made it happen.'

'Speaking of fathers,' George added softly, 'have you spoken with Andrew?'

Melissa shook her head and opened her handbag to retrieve her phone. She panicked when she couldn't find it and wracked her brain to remember when she last called somebody.

'I think it's on the kitchen table at Currumbin. I haven't used it since Monday, when I called you to let you know I'd arrived safely. I've gotta go get it.'

'Will you come straight back?'

Melissa paused. 'No. I'll come down tomorrow with Ben. We'll come here to the house so we can go to the church together.'

'Don't be late. And please, let Ben drive.'

'I will. I promise.'

*M*elissa's mobile phone was sitting on the kitchen table under a large piece of paper with the words, *Here Tis*. Ben's humour. She checked her messages. Four calls. One from her father, one from Karen and two from Andrew.

Message one: 'Call me as soon as you arrive darling.'

Message two: 'Good to see you today Melissa. Pleased you told me about the accident and your baby. Ben will be at your funeral on behalf of everyone here at Niche. Although of course we are the only two who know. Don't forget to reach out to me – at any time.'

. . .

Message three: 'Melissa it's Andrew. Ummm. I hate voice mail. I'll call later.'

Message four: 'It's me again. The eloquent one. Sorry for the last message. I hope you're doing OK. Gosh I want to see you. I need to talk to you. I've been delayed here in Perth by a day — but should be home Thursday evening. I'll be there for you on Friday.'

Melissa pressed redial on the phone.

'Melissa,' she heard Andrew reply quickly, before an airport announcement interrupted him.

'This is a final boarding call for QF 594 to Brisbane. Can all remaining passengers please board. Passengers are reminded that they cannot use electronic devices once they have left the departure hall.'

'Can't talk now. Gotta go. I'm pleased you called. Tomorrow ... I'll see you tomorrow.'

'OK,' she replied quickly. 'Tomorrow.'

Melissa put the phone on charge and wrote herself a message to remember to take it tomorrow. There was the sound of a key in the front door and Ben walked in.

'Good to see ya Mel,' he offered with a cheeky smile. They hugged like football players.

'Oops,' she gasped, 'gotta call dad.'

The sun streamed in through Melissa's window on Friday morning. It doesn't feel right for today to be bright and sunny, Melissa reflected while sitting on her bed pulling on her black turtleneck, skirt and boots. She was tired and could hear Ben crashing around in the kitchen making tea and toast. Melissa waved away the toast he offered as she walked into the kitchen and disconnected her phone from the charger. She felt like she was on autopilot. Ben walked over to her with a mug of tea.

'Hug then mug,' he said softly.

She smiled, let herself be embraced and then took a sip of the tea he offered. Sitting down, she pressed play on her phone and watched again the video of her son's last moments. She pulled out the eulogy to check that it had captured all she wanted to say. Ben looked at her.

'May I?' he asked.

Melissa passed the eulogy over. He read it in silence and then looked at her.

'Yep. You got it.'

Melissa stared out of the window and said nothing on the drive down to Bangalow. Her father was sitting at the kitchen table with Helen, looking at the photos Andrew had taken. He stood up and embraced her.

'Have you eaten, love?' he asked.

Ben was standing behind her, shaking his head, and Helen went to the kitchen to bring over sandwiches. There was a knock at the door, and George let the funeral director in. Melissa took a deep breath and shivered.

In Brisbane, Andrew was anxious to get to the funeral. He had slept through his alarm after a late arrival into Brisbane airport Thursday evening. Slow moving traffic on the Pacific Highway was increasing his anxiety by the minute. He tapped on the steering wheel impatiently and looked at his watch.

Melissa walked into the church on her father's arm. She gasped when she saw the tiny white casket at the front of the church. His death was so real, so final and so unfair.

Andrew parked the car hard up against the curb and ran until he was in the foyer of the church. A hymn was playing so he paused to catch his breath. On a table besides the entrance was a framed photo of Melissa and the baby. He smiled. An image of love. It was the photo he had taken at the hospital that dreadful Saturday nearly two weeks ago. His eyes ran down the aisle and he could see the tiny white casket at the front overflowing with flowers. There shouldn't be a need for caskets this size. He looked to the left and saw Melissa standing between Ben and her father, with Helen the other side of George. In the second row his father was standing beside Doctor McDonald, with his three brothers in the row behind. Miles saw him and waved for him to join them. He took his place beside his brother. It had only been eight months since he was last here, standing beside Miles for his mother's funeral.

The hymn finished and the small party of mourners sat. The minister announced that there would be a eulogy. There were whispered discussions in the front row, before Ben stood up and walked behind the pulpit.

'I have a letter here for Scott from Melissa.'

If I had to bury my son,
I would hope that I was one hundred and ten
And that he had enjoyed the rich life he deserved.
And that standing here today
I would have wonderful stories to share
Of sandcastles built and races run along the beach.

But this was not to be your story.
My heart is breaking
That all I have to share with you
Is knowledge of how much you were loved.

I want you to know
That I was waiting for you
Your room was nearly ready
And that I had already briefed you
while you were in my womb
On all the things we were going to do together.

It was going to be a wonderful life.

But now I need to find a new path
Without you on this journey
I'll never forget you
And will think of you every day
And I hope that each time you hear
The roar of thunder and rain falling to the earth
That you will remember
That these are my tears
Flowing into a never-ending river of love for you.

Ben finished the eulogy and walked over to the casket and placed the letter under the flowers. He returned to his seat and put his arm around Melissa. Andrew ached. He wished he was there beside her. Everyone in the small congregation was sniffling and scrambling for tissues. The minister took his place again behind the lectern.

'He only lived a day, but he was very loved. Melissa

would like to thank you all for coming today to celebrate his life and to support her. Scott Andrew George Brinkley is now gone from our lives but will remain in our memories and in our hearts forever. Please stand to join me for our final hymn.'

Andrew started shaking.

'Scott Andrew ...', he ran the words over again in his head. Scott *was* his son – and his son was dead.

He was suddenly aware that everyone was standing, and that Miles was looking at him. He stood slowly, looked at his brother, shook his head and walked out of the church. Once outside, he ran to his car and turned on the ignition. He did a quick U-turn and drove out of town, not noticing that his brother had chased him. He was on autopilot driving with no destination in mind. He noticed that his knuckles on the steering wheel were white. Recognising his stress, he pulled off the road at McLeod Shoot. He remained in the car, looking down across the mountain range towards Byron Bay. But he didn't see the beauty. All he could see was Melissa's broken car and the image of her holding their tiny broken son.

Knock knock. Andrew's thoughts were interrupted by someone tapping on the passenger side window of the car. He looked up and saw Miles so unlocked the car. Miles climbed inside and shut the door quietly behind him.

'So. You're a father,' Miles said softly.

'Was a father,' Andrew replied dryly. 'She didn't tell me.'

'She's had a lot to deal with, and I guess she was trying not to disrupt your life and your relationship with Kate,' Miles responded.

Andrew shook his head.

'What a mess. What a horrible, horrible mess I've made of everything. I feel so ...,' he hesitated. 'I'm just ... I don't know what I am. I'm ... I'm overwhelmed I guess. I'm three parts angry. Two parts sad. Deeply sad ... So much loss. And there's love ...'

'She's clearly more to you than *just* the girl next door,' Miles offered.

'We've been friends forever. And *obviously* more than that more recently. But I've stuffed up. Big time. I may've missed my chance. I don't know what Ben is to her. What if he's more than a house mate.'

'You need to find out bro, and at the very least you need to be there for her. To help her get through this. She's had a truly horrible year. And maybe by helping her, you'll help yourself.'

Andrew said nothing as he watched another car pull up and a couple get out of their car to admire the scenery. They were chatting animatedly taking selfies with the view in the background. There was clearly lightness and laughter in their relationship and Andrew grieved for this in his relationship with Melissa.

'I'll speak to her,' Andrew announced suddenly. 'Thanks for coming, Miles.'

His brother nodded and got out of the car.

❦

Melissa barely remembered walking out of the church between her father and Ben, and getting into the funeral director's car. The image of the tiny white coffin was her only focus and tears streamed down her face. Everything else was a blur. She hated leaving him and the reality of his death hit her like a blow to the head from a baseball bat. He was gone. He was really gone. She thought of his tiny blue bonnet under her pillow back in Currumbin and she became anxious. Helen placed a cup of tea in front of her, but she shook her head. Someone sat down beside her and she looked up to see that it was Doctor McDonald.

'I'm very worried about you,' she said simply. 'I've been calling your dad every other day to see how you were. I ... I ...' the doctor struggled for words. 'I can't even begin to imagine how difficult today was for you. But, you did it. Another step. A very difficult one on an incredibly difficult journey. You probably won't remember, but here is my card. Please call me. You need to talk to someone about your grief.'

Melissa picked up the card and touched the doctor's hand. The doctor left and Melissa walked over to Ben.

'Can you take me back to Currumbin?'

'Of course,' he replied.

Melissa walked over to her father and wrapped her arms around him.

'Dad, I've got to go. I can't stay. It's ... it's too hard. Ben will be with me.'

'Oh darling. I don't think so. Are you sure?'

'I'm not sure of anything. I just want to go back to Currumbin for now.'

George watched Ben support Melissa out to his car. Moments later they were gone.

Andrew knocked on George Bourne's front door. He opened the door and spoke before Andrew had time to say anything.

'She's gone son. Ben has driven her back to Currumbin.'

*A*ndrew arrived at Melissa's house shortly after 6.00pm. He tentatively knocked on the door knowing that Ben would be there having seen two cars in the driveway. Ben opened the door.

'I've been expecting you,' he said matter-of-factly. 'She's out the back on the swing. I'm heading off to Brisbane. Won't be back 'til Sunday. Look after her. Please.'

Ben picked up his keys and overnight bag and walked past Andrew before he had a chance to reply. Andrew watched him leave, closed the front door, walked through the house and out the back door to the garden. Melissa was rocking herself on the swing. She barely acknowledged his arrival. Her eyes were transfixed on a tiny bundle of wool in her hands: the blue bonnet. He sat down on one of the iron chairs two metres away from her. It was dark and chilly. The shortest day of the year, the winter solstice, had just passed. Andrew wondered if the darkest day for them had passed as well. He listened to the creek and the sounds of the birds calling out to each other.

He looked at Melissa, staring at the bonnet.

'Why didn't you tell me?' he asked softly.

This was not how he planned to start the conversation and he wanted to draw back the words as soon as they were spoken.

'I'm sorry,' she whispered without looking up.

He looked at his hands and then back at her.

'The eulogy was beautiful,' he offered, trying a more positive approach. He was in a situation in which he had no experience.

She nodded, but didn't say anything and continued staring at the bonnet while rocking on the swing.

'Can I get you anything?' Andrew asked tentatively.

She shook her head.

'You're shivering,' he said, and walked back into the house to retrieve a small blanket from the sofa. He returned and gently placed the blanket over her shoulders, sitting down beside her on the swing. Melissa barely acknowledged him. He reached out to touch the bonnet and their hands brush against each other.

'May I?' he asked gesturing towards the bonnet.

Melissa nodded and released the bonnet. Andrew brought the bonnet to his cheek and felt its softness. He drew circles on his cheek with the tiny, precious bundle.

Melissa watched him doing the same thing she had done a hundred times: connecting to her son through his tiny woollen hat.

'This is all we've left of him,' Andrew said sombrely.

'We have the photos, the lovely photos you took of him at the hospital,' Melissa offered. 'So precious. And there are the memories of him moving in my womb.'

'But those are your memories. You didn't share them with me.' Andrew stood up suddenly feeling agitated. 'You should have told me. He was my son too. I've missed all those moments in my son's short life.'

Melissa looked at Andrew seeing anger in his eyes.

'I'm sorry. I'm so sorry. I messed up. I was...' Melissa's voice trailed off as she started to cry.

Guilt washed over Andrew. He sat down again beside her on the swing as her pain released a thundering water-fall of tears. She leant into him sobbing, and Andrew wrapped his arms around her feeling her frailty.

'Let's go inside, out of the cold,' he suggested.

Melissa struggled to stand up and slipped on the damp grass as she started to walk. Andrew caught her before she fell, scooped her up in his arms and carried her inside to her bedroom. He lay her gently on the bed and took off her damp sneakers. Removing his shoes, he laid down behind her, pulling the blanket over them both. He put his arm over her, snuggled in close so that their bodies were one and hugged her until she stopped sobbing and finally fell asleep. Andrew lay very still, listening to her breathing. He soaked in the scent of her hair and treasured this feeling of closeness. Listening to the sounds outside from Currumbin Creek, he eventually fell asleep as well.

Around midnight, Melissa woke up with a start. She was thirsty and momentarily disoriented. There was a shaft of light shining in the bedroom from a street lamp. Andrew's hand was covering hers and she examined all the ridges and folds in detail. She could feel his breath against her neck and the weight of his arm on her waist. Feeling cocooned she was reluctant to disturb him. But she was thirsty. She gently lifted his arm, kissed his hand and slid out from his embrace. Her socked feet cushioned the sound of her footsteps on the way to the kitchen. On her return up the hall she noticed Ben wasn't in his room and wondered when he had left.

Andrew had not moved. She looked at him sleeping and remembered their night together in Brisbane. Without thinking, she took off her clothes and slid under the blanket beside him. She lay facing him examining his hair and his eyes and the clavicle bones around his neck. Every part of him up close was special, and she reached out and gently stroked his chest. Andrew opened his eyes. He was surprised to see Melissa looking at him and that her fingers were now pushing at the buttons on his shirt.

'What are you doing...?' he asked.

Melissa said nothing and continued fiddling with his buttons. Andrew moved his hand and was surprised to feel her flesh. He pulled the blanket off to see that she was naked.

Her body was splattered with a kaleidoscope of coloured bruises from reddish blue to purplish black. And there was a scar on her midriff where their son entered the world. His eyes filled with tears as he regarded the impact of the accident.

'Shhh,' Melissa cooed while she continued to undo the buttons on his shirt.

He ran his hand over her hip and across the scar.

He got off the bed to remove his shirt and trousers all the while looking at her, looking at him. Now naked, he knelt on the bed and reached across to kiss her scar. Ever so gently, he kissed inside the curve of her hip and then her breast before he took her nipple in his mouth. Melissa groaned at the pleasurable feelings building in her body, as his teeth tugged at each nipple, she shivered and came. No words were uttered as they clung to each other in a tight embrace, feeling relieved that they had found a way back to each other.

*a*ndrew was woken by a dozen rosellas noisily chasing each other through the bottlebrush tree outside the bedroom window. Melissa was still sleeping and he dared not move in case he woke her. He looked at her face in the morning light. A buzzing noise distracted him. It was his phone. He quickly slid out of bed and took his phone to the kitchen. 'Kate' was showing clearly on the display. He hesitated to answer for just a moment, and then, remembered that today was the day they were meant to be getting married. He answered the call.

'Kate – is everything OK?' he answered softly.

'OK. Is everything OK you ask. Where are you?' Kate demanded. 'Are you with her?'

He was struck by the odd tone in her voice. Something was not right. This was not the calm and rational Kate he knew.

'Is anyone with you Kate?' Andrew replied without answering her question.

'Why would anyone be here? It's not like I'm getting married today or anything.'

'Kate, can you sit down for me. Please. Have you taken something?' he asked tentatively.

'Why would you care if I had? I'm not your responsibility,' she responded tersely.

'When was the last time you spoke with your parents?'

No response.

'Kate. Kate. Listen to me. I'm worried about you. I still care for you. I'm coming.'

'Whatever,' she responded strangely before hanging up.

Andrew rushed back to the bedroom to get dressed. Melissa woke up as he was putting on his shoes.

'Leaving me?' she whispered.

'I'm sorry. I'm so sorry. Kate just called. I think she's taken something. I'm worried. Very worried. And I'm responsible. I've got to go to Brisbane to see her. But I don't want you to stay here on your own. Can you go to your Dad's today? Please. Go to Bangalow. She nodded. Andrew jumped back on the bed and hugged Melissa tightly. He looked into her eyes and kissed her gently. Then he kissed her again, this time with all the passion that'd been bottled up for months. Breaking from their embrace he looked at her.

'I don't want to go. I don't want to leave you. But I have to. I'm sorry. What a mess I've made of things. I'll call you when I'm clearer about what's going on.'

Melissa reached up and kissed him on the forehead.

'Go,' she said simply.

Andrew climbed off the bed, scooped up his jacket and left. Melissa listened to the car driving away before getting out of bed. The house was eerily quiet.

JUNE 23 – LATE MORNING

*A*ndrew called Kate's father before leaving Currumbin. The phone went through to voicemail.

'Marcus. It's Andrew. I've just had a call from Kate. I'm worried. I'm on my way there now. I know it's not like her, but I think she's been drinking. Good if you could be there too.'

He arrived at Kate's apartment in Brisbane an hour later. He opened the door and found her sitting on the floor beside a crumpled wedding dress and several empty wine bottles. She didn't look up.

'Kate,' he whispered softly as he sat down on the floor beside her. 'Are you OK?'

'I'm worthless.'

Andrew was shocked by her response.

'Oh Kate. You're not worthless.'

'And I'm alone,'

'I'm here. You're not alone.'

'But you don't love me anymore.'

Andrew put his arm around her and pulled her close, unsure of what to say. He looked at the empty bottles.

'Have you taken anything?'

She didn't respond. Andrew got up and walked to the kitchen. On the kitchen table, in the middle of a dozen photos of them both, was an empty bottle of paracetamol.

'How many of these did you take?'

'I'm not sure,' she said, looking at him with vacant eyes.

A key turning in the lock at the front door caught Andrew's attention. Marcus and Heather Williams entered the apartment, their faces deeply creased, reflecting their concern. Kate's mother rushed over to her daughter, kneeling beside her on the floor.

'We thought she was OK. She seemed fine, taking your deferred engagement very well,' Marcus directed at Andrew with no small sense of irony.

'So did I. I had no idea she was feeling ...' his voice trailed off. 'I'm going to call the ambulance. I don't know what she's taken, but she's not herself.'

Two ambulance officers were in the apartment ten minutes later loading Kate onto a trolley.

'We'll take her to the Royal Brisbane Hospital – to get her checked out.'

Marcus and Heather followed the ambulance out and

Andrew signalled that he would follow them over shortly. He called Melissa and left a message on her voicemail.

'I'm on my way to the hospital. We're not sure what Kate has taken. She's in good hands now but...' his voice trailed off. 'I'll wait with her parents until we know more. I'll call as soon as I can. Oh and ...' Andrew paused again, 'and I forgot to tell you I loved waking up beside you this morning. I want to do that more often.'

George Bourne was surprised and delighted to see his daughter driving up his driveway. He walked down the front steps and greeted her with a warm embrace as she got out of the car.

'How are you love?'

Melissa looked at her father while she thought about how to respond.

'I've made my bed, cooked breakfast and driven safely down to see you. I think that's something.

Her father hugged her again.

'Andrew not with you?' he asked.

'No. He's in Brisbane. Kate's having difficulty dealing with their breakup. Serious difficulty,' she added with emphasis.

'Oh dear. Yes, of course. Today was meant to be *their* big day – wasn't it?' George sighed. 'Anyway, come inside, I have my own news to share.'

Melissa sat down at the kitchen table while he prepared a pot of tea.

'You're not spending the day with Helen?' she asked a little cheekily.

'She'll be here shortly. In fact, she's going to be here quite a bit, because ...,' he paused for effect, 'we're getting married.'

'Goodness, Dad! Really? She's very nice but you've only known her for what ... two weeks?'

'Yep, two weeks. I was fairly sure that I wanted to spend every day of the rest of my life with her after two days. But I didn't want to rush things. And then I thought, well with the accident, and knowing how precious every day was, I asked her to marry me. And strike me down, she said yes. So, there you have it. We're having a celebratory lunch today and we'd love it if you joined us.'

Melissa hugged her father.

'That's lovely Dad. Just lovely. I'm so happy for you both.'

Suddenly they were both crying and smiling and enjoying the moment.

'So when's the big day?'

'Next Saturday. Here in the home paddock. Are you free?'

Melissa laughed and hugged her father again.

'Yes of course,' she replied.

Footsteps in the hallway got their attention. Helen

had arrived with a basket loaded with food. She smiled at them both.

'So Helen, when are you and I going dress shopping?'

'Is Monday good for you?'

'Absolutely,' Melissa said as she walked over to give her a hug. 'Congratulations. It's hard for me to describe how happy I am. This is super news.'

'It's the mermaid,' cried a voice from the hall. All eyes turned to Scott, who walked over to Melissa, carrying several books.

'Read to me?' he asked hopefully.

'Of course,' she said. 'Which one first?'

'*Finding Nemo*,' he said, trying to crawl on to her lap. Melissa lifted him up.

'Goodness, Scott. You're heavy. I think you've been eating way too many jelly fish.'

Scott giggled and opened the first page expectantly.

Several difficult hours had dragged by in the waiting room at the Royal Brisbane Hospital. Tension between Kate's parents and Andrew was felt in every conversation. The doctor had undertaken a number of tests and reported that Kate was lucky not to have received serious damage to her liver and kidneys. By midday, Kate was coherent. She apologised profusely to her parents for the trouble she'd caused and explained that she had had a splitting headache from having consumed too much wine. The paracetamol was taken to stop the pain, although she couldn't remember how many tablets she had taken. The doctor indicated that she would be kept overnight for observation and that if he was satisfied she was well enough, would release her the following day. Relieved, Andrew left the hospital, knowing Kate's parents would be there with her for the rest of the day. He promised to return tomorrow and drove back to his apartment on Queen Street in the city.

Melissa had read three books to Scott before Helen announced that it was time to put them away for lunch. There was frequent laughter while they ate and Melissa couldn't remember such a happy day spent with her father in a long time. After dessert, Melissa proposed a toast.

'To Dad and Helen. Just so pleased you found each other. All the best for next Saturday and every other day that follows.'

'Chin chin,' offered Scott, lifting his glass of water up so quickly that half of it splashed on his face and hair.

'You really do love the water, don't you?' Helen said smiling broadly. 'We'll do some more splashing on the beach this afternoon.'

'Yippee,' Scott squealed. 'Will you be coming?' he asked Melissa.

'Why of course,' she said, affectionately brushing some of the water off his face.

Melissa checked her phone messages while her father cleared the plates. She smiled when she heard Andrew's message about wanting to wake up beside her more often. Yesterday had been so emotionally difficult. Saying goodbye to her son was something she had never imagined having to do. Being intimate with Andrew was a way of smothering the pain, if only for a short while. Feelings of melancholy returned.

'You're sad?' Scott offered, looking intently at her face.

'Well, not when I'm around you,' she said pushing the fringe from his eyes.

Melissa drove her father down to Byron Bay while Helen drove Scott. They'd agreed to rendezvous with Scott's parents in Clarkes Beach car park around three o'clock. Melissa enjoyed the time alone with her father on the drive down to The Bay.

'Well, Dad. Getting married. Wow. I'm just so pleased for you both.'

'Thanks love. You being happy about this is important to us.'

'There's going to be lots to do in the coming week. Let me know how I can help.'

'You're very kind offer is accepted, although I think we have most things sorted out. Won't be a big affair but there's likely to be things to chase up that we'd not thought about. For the moment, if you could help with the invitation distribution. I'll leave you to look after inviting all the Wyatt men.'

Melissa smiled.

'Of course Dad.'

It was a lovely winter's afternoon and there were a few surfers braving the chilly water to ride the long and gentle waves at Clarkes Beach. There were also a number of small boys playing on the water's edge and Scott rushed to join them.

'I'll be down in a moment Dad,' Melissa held up her phone to indicate she'd be making a call. Her father nodded and carried two folding chairs down the narrow path to the beach to join Helen.

Andrew answered the phone on the second ring.

'Hello there. How are you?'

'Good. I'm good. I'm looking out over beautiful Clarkes Beach and for the moment,' she paused, 'everything is calm in my world. I slept really well last night. And I woke up in the arms of someone I care about a great deal.'

'I see,' he said in a slightly professorial tone, delighted by her comment.

'And I would be very open to repeating the experience.'

'Which bit would you like to repeat? Would that be the good night's sleep, or the waking up in someone's arms?' he asked cautiously.

'Hmmmm,' she replied. 'I'll need to think about that. Both bits were lovely.'

The phone line went quiet while they reflected on what wasn't being said.

Melissa coughed as if to break the moment. 'How's Kate?'

'Better. She said she accidentally took too many paracetamol as she was in a lot of pain. This could be the truth, but we're not sure. The doctor will make an assessment today as to whether she can go home. I need to be there for that – and for her. I'm responsible and I can't abandon her. Do you understand?'

'Of course. Take the time that you need – that she needs,' Melissa responded quietly.

'Thank you. I hate being away from you and I want to be there for you.'

'I know. We'll have time, we'll make time. And there's an event I'd like you to attend. A wedding ...' Melissa paused for effect.

'A wedding ...' Andrew responded tentatively.

'Yes, my father is marrying Helen Harmon next Saturday and the entire Wyatt family is invited.'

'Wow, really? That was quick! Mind you, who am I to judge.' Andrew stopped, thinking about what he'd just said. He was very aware he and Kate got engaged after knowing each other for only two weeks – so hardly a good example of a quick engagement. He continued, 'That's wonderful news. Of course I'll be there. Can you tell them I accept, with pleasure? I'm sure Dad will call round this evening with a bottle of something red to celebrate.'

'I will,' she said laughing.

Neither said anything for a moment. It was an easy silence knowing the other was still there.

'So,' he said, 'you're going to have a busy week, getting ready for Saturday.'

'Probably. It's just so lovely being around a father who is *so* happy. It makes my own pain a little easier to bear.'

'Melissa, I wish ... I wish,' Andrew said stumbling on his words, 'I wish I could take away your pain.'

'Thank you,' she whispered.

'Mermaid, come here,' Scott cried out from the path to the beach, interrupting their conversation.

'Mermaid?' Andrew asked, 'who's calling you a mermaid?'

She laughed. 'There's someone you need to meet. He's actually Helen's grandson although I didn't know this when I met him here at the beach last year. He made such an impression that I named our son after him. He's curious and loves being read to, and he ...' her voice trailed off, 'he's just lovely, even though he constantly makes me think of our Scott.'

There was silence again on the phone. A car pulled into the car park, and a couple got out and waved to Helen who had just emerged at the top of the path from the beach.

'Scott's parents have just arrived. I have to go. I promise I'll call again soon, and I look forward to seeing you Saturday.'

'Me too. Keep safe. Miss you.'

Helen introduced Melissa to her son, Louis, and his wife, Jenny.

*a*ndrew met with Kate's parents and the doctor at the hospital the following morning.

'I've spoken with Kate. She's feeling much better and her vital signs are good. However, I'm concerned about her reluctance to talk about what she was thinking on Friday night when she consumed alcohol and paracetamol together. She seems too calm and rational, although I don't know her very well. I'd be reluctant for her to be on her own until we're sure she's fine. I'm happy to release her as long as you can arrange for someone to be with her.'

'I can be there for her during the day,' Andrew offered immediately. 'I'm on vacation this week and can arrive in the morning and stay until you both come home from work,' he said, talking directly to Kate's parents. 'We need time to talk, and we'll have plenty of it.'

'She'll probably think she's being mollycoddled,' Heather Williams remarked.

'I expect so,' her father replied. 'But I have no problem doing this until we're sure she's OK.'

'Good,' said the doctor. 'I'll sign her out.'

George's house was a hive of activity on Sunday morning. George was discussing his slashing and mowing needs with William Wyatt while Helen and Melissa explored floral and lighting arrangements. Lists were written and checked and friends and neighbours were called to see if they were available at late notice for a wedding. All the activity meant there were parts of the day when Melissa wasn't thinking about Scott or Andrew.

Monday was also busy, with Helen taking her to the best dress shops between Bangalow, Byron Bay and Ballina. They had a lovely time, chatting while they modelled outfits for each other. Ben called as they were wrapping up their shopping for the day.

'How are you Mel?' he asked tentatively.

'I'm good. I've had a good day. Thanks for asking.'

'What are you doing?'

'Shopping for wedding dresses,' Melissa replied.

There was silence on Ben's end of the phone.

'My dad's marrying the *lovely Helen Harmon* next

Saturday,' she said looking at Helen. 'You've very welcome to come along. Are you free?'

'Nope. I'll be surfing at Ellis Beach in far north Queensland next weekend, with mates from Uni – won't be back 'til Monday.'

'Ah well. I'll be sure to bore you with all the photos,' Melissa said, still smiling at Helen. 'And you Ben? How are things with you?'

'Awesome actually. Niche just won three new jobs down at The Bay because the bloke you did the designs for at Wategos Beach was so chuffed he's been telling everybody. I've already volunteered to be a part of any team working there. And while I think about it, we're having a special morning tea at the office to celebrate on Friday. If you felt up to it, might be a good way for you to come back to work slowly.'

Melissa took a moment to gather her thoughts before replying. 'OK. I'll be there. Can you tell Karen? But just for the celebration on Friday. I'll start work full time the following week.'

'Great news! Just so pleased to have you back.'

Helen and Melissa placed their purchases in the boot of the car and headed back to Bangalow.

They sat in a companionable silence for a few minutes until Melissa spoke.

'Helen I just wanted to let you know how thrilled I am about you and Dad. You've made him so happy.'

'Well, you know that goes both ways. He's a lovely man and I'm very lucky to have met him. I've been lonely too since Jack died three years ago. Volunteering at the hospital has helped me. I really do feel that in helping others, you help yourself.'

'So where are you and Dad going to live? Bangalow or Byron Bay?'

'We'll spend most of our time at Bangalow I expect, although I'll continue to volunteer at the hospital two days a week – and I also have child minding commitments – that I would *never surrender*.'

Melissa smiled at Helen's emphasis.

'Completely understand. You have an adorable grandson. Now here's a thought for you, I was just speaking with Ben, who will probably be working at The Bay for a couple of months. If you're open to having a lodger I'm sure he would accept. Might be good to have someone at the house when you're in Bangalow.'

'That sounds like a mutually beneficial arrangement. Keep me posted.'

Andrew collected Kate at 8:30am and they spent the day walking beside the river in the centre of Brisbane. They talked while they walked, but the conversation was always light, with resistance from Kate to revealing anything about how she was feeling on Friday evening. He didn't push her and they spent several hours sitting on a bench in the botanical gardens, watching the ferries ploughing up and down the river. It was an easy way to spend time together but Andrew knew that Kate wouldn't be able to move forward until she had dealt with her underlying feelings. It was not until the third day of walking and sitting and watching that Kate began to open up.

'Thank you for coming on Saturday. I'm sorry that ...' her voice trailed off. 'This is hard for me. It's as though you've died and I'm still grieving for you – for us. It's not real you being here now. It's only temporary. Soon you'll be gone and I'll be alone again.'

Andrew closed his eyes feeling the pain in her words.

'I'm sorry. I wish I could say sorry one hundred times and you would feel better. I hate the way I've made you feel. I hate that by admitting I still loved Melissa I made you feel unworthy. That was so unfair on you. You're so beautiful and so worthy of someone to love you. I wish I'd known not to rush into our relationship until I was ... I don't know... until I was sure I could start again. But I didn't know myself. Like you, I was feeling rejected and unworthy and I guess that made me vulnerable to loving someone else before I was ready. I should have given myself time to mourn.'

'I don't want to get over you Andrew. I don't want to

mourn the loss of you of our relationship and of the wonderful future we were going to have together.'

Andrew sighed.

'I'm sorry. It's over, and there's nothing I can say to make it better. I know mourning is hard and our instinct is to avoid it. Mourning is tough, and it's natural to try to avoid it. But we can't. We have to work through it. We have to face it. I know, because I've lost my son and I only knew him for the briefest of moments. I've...' Andrew's voice croaked and he stopped talking. He stood up, walked over to the river bank and took a deep breath. Kate walked over to him and put her hand on his shoulder.

'I didn't know. I'm sorry.'

'I didn't know myself for sure until the funeral. I feel cheated that I didn't know and had so little time with him.'

'I imagine Melissa is struggling.'

He nodded. 'Yes. We all manage loss in different ways. She recognises that she has a long journey ahead and she'll probably *never* get over the loss of her son – of our son.'

'I was thinking the same thing Friday night. If I was never going to get over losing you, was there any point in continuing to be in pain and carrying on? I thought it might be best if I went to sleep and didn't wake up the next morning. Except that I did wake up and I felt worse... much worse... and then I called you.'

Andrew turned around and held Kate while she quietly started to weep.

Thursday's walk together was more positive with their conversation turning to the future. After much discussion Kate decided she was going to investigate getting a job in Europe and spend time travelling and working. Her company had an office in London, so a transfer was possible although she would prefer a break from everything that was familiar.

'I think time out for reflection and an environment with new people and possibilities might help,' Andrew offered.

'I hope so. And for you?' she asked, 'What does the future hold for you?'

'I'm not sure yet, but I'm hopeful Melissa will be a part of it. Which part, I'm not sure.'

Andrew was invited to dinner at the Williams' home on Thursday night. It was an evening full of lively conversation and laughter, with a recognition beneath the surface that this was the last time the four of them would be together. There were long hugs as Andrew said goodbye to Marcus and Heather. On Friday morning, Andrew and

Kate went for their last walk along the river. They walked easily, reflecting on things they had done together during the past six months. By the time Andrew dropped Kate back at her parent's place there was nothing left to be said. Except goodbye. They hugged briefly and Andrew kissed her hair.

'I wish you nothing but happiness Kate. You deserve it.'

He got in the car and drove away without looking back.

On Friday, Melissa arrived at the Niche offices at 3:00pm. She was excited and nervous in equal measure so sat in the car for a few minutes mentally preparing herself for the inevitable questions she would be asked about the accident. Ben saw her from the office window and came out.

'Are you OK?'

Melissa shook her head.

'It'll be fine. I'll be there for you,' he said.

Melissa nodded, got out of the car and came inside. She negotiated her way through hugs and smiles on her way to the office boardroom where a celebratory after-noon tea had been laid out. The Niche team were in good spirits and there was a high volume of chatter.

'Shhh,' Karen announced, before tapping a teaspoon

on the side of a teacup to get everyone's attention.

'What a great day. We have much to celebrate and delighted to have the entire team here.'

She smiled at Melissa. 'As you know, we've picked up three new projects in Byron Bay in addition to a number of extension projects in Surfers Paradise. Always great to have a solid pipeline of work and important to take time out to recognise these milestone moments. Thank you everyone, with a special shout out to Melissa, whose excellent work was instrumental in us getting recommended for a few of these projects. Thank you everybody.'

There was a spontaneous round of applause.

'And I'm also delighted to report that Melissa has agreed to join Niche as a permanent employee, starting Monday.'

More applause and cheering with Ben's cries of support being heard above all others.

Melissa looked round the room at her colleagues. She felt appreciated and safe in this group so decided to say a few words.

'Thank you Karen and indeed thank you everyone. I'm delighted to be back at work, after a pretty awful couple of weeks.' Everyone looked cautiously at Melissa. 'As I think most of you know, I was in a car accident and ...' Melissa paused, 'while my body is mending slowly, my heart was damaged.' Her colleagues look at each other, concerned.

'This is difficult for me. But you need to know that I am in mourning for my not-yet-ready to be born son who died as a result of the accident.' Several women caught their breath. 'Wow, I've said it.' She paused again. 'I've finally been able to say those terrible words and to recognise my loss. I want to be back at work and to take steps towards a normal life, but I will need for you to be patient with me as it's going to take me a while to get used to Scott not being a part of my life. That's all. Thank you for your understanding.'

There was silence for a moment followed by an enthusiastic round of applause.

Karen walked over and hugged Melissa, while several women pulled handkerchiefs from their bags.

Ben wrapped his arms around Melissa once Karen released her.

'That was perfect Mel.'

A queue had formed behind Ben, with every member of the team wanting to share a private word with Melissa. Ben stepped aside, but stayed protectively nearby. He was concerned about the emotional toll the conversations would have. He needn't have worried, as Melissa seemed to draw strength from talking to others about her loss. At 4:30pm she nodded at Ben to let him know that she was ready to leave. He walked her out to the car and gave her a final hug.

'Step by step,' she said softly.

*W*edding day arrived crisp, bright and clear. Melissa was astonished at the transformation that had taken place in her father's home paddock. There were bottles with flowers hanging from the jacaranda and poinciana trees with their trunks embraced in hundreds of tiny white lights. A pergola had been threaded with white and pink roses, making a stunning setting for the wedding vows, and there was a large tent with a timber floor and small tables decorated with white tablecloths, candles and flowers. Melissa thought that it was a magical setting and was surprised at the obvious attention and affection that her father and Helen had invested in planning the day. She dressed early so she could help her father get ready. Her emerald satin dress was accompanied by a crepe jacket of the same length and she wore the antique bracelet that had belonged to Andrew's mother.

'You sparkle honey,' her father whispered in her ear as she adjusted the rose in his button hole.

There were thirty cars parked tightly in the driveway by 2:30pm, with most seats facing the pergola occupied by 2:45. The five Wyatt men, who had the shortest distance to travel across the paddocks and over the small bridge at Byron Creek, arrived at two minutes to three, taking the last five seats in the back row. Melissa greeted them all as she walked to the front to take her seat. She beamed as she looked at the obvious love in her father's eyes.

Louis Harmon slowly walked his mother down the steps of the house, and between friends and family seated on either side of the red carpet. Helen wore a beautiful light-grey satin dress with lace overlay and elbow length jacket, while her father wore a grey suit with the light pink rose in his button hole that Melissa had lovingly placed. By 3:30pm vows had been exchanged and the marriage celebrant had declared Helen Harmon and George Bourne husband and wife. Champagne corks started popping, and drinks and canapés were served. Andrew watched Melissa move easily among the crowd, delighting to see the re-emergence of her confidence.

'You Wyatt boys scrub up well,' she said approaching Andrew, Miles and William.

'Not half as well as you,' William offered, leaning in to give her a kiss on the cheek. 'You look gorgeous.'

'Thank you for the compliment and for the excellent job in taming the grass in the home paddock.'

William and Miles walked over to the next table to join their father, who was chatting with Doctor McDonald, leaving Andrew and Melissa alone.

'I was going to say you took my breath away – but you literally *took my breath away*.'

'Well you need to tell Helen. She chose my dress.'

Andrew smiled still admiring the dress.

'How did your week with Kate go? Is she better?'

'I think,' Andrew paused, 'she's going to be OK. It'll take time though. We had a couple of difficult conversations and I think she accepts my problem was that I never got over you. It had nothing to do with her.'

He paused and took a sip of champagne.

'She's going overseas. We've said goodbye now, so that chapter is over.'

He looked into Melissa's eyes and was about to speak, when the band started playing. Andrew's brother Neil was the Master of Ceremonies for the evening and called for everyone to welcome Mr and Mrs Bourne to the dance floor for the bridal waltz. Helen and George walked to the centre of the tent as the band struck up a beautiful rendition of *Fly Me to The Moon*. The lead singer belted out the opening lyrics with gusto. One minute later other dancers were encouraged to join. Andrew was amused to see his father escorting Doctor McDonald to the dance floor. He couldn't remember ever seeing his father dance. Andrew smiled and looked at Melissa. The song ended and the band transitioned to, *Something About the Way You Look Tonight*.

'This song was written for you. Will you dance with me?'

Melissa nodded and moved easily into Andrew's arms. Neither noticed Helen and George sharing a conspiratorial look. Melissa leant into Andrew and he pulled her close. He stroked her back and breathed in the scent of her. They looked at each other and smiled.

'Isn't this lovely,' Andrew started, but was interrupted by Miles, asking if he could dance with Melissa.

'Sorry bro. Nope. She's all mine tonight.'

Miles smiled and moved away. The song ended and Andrew held Melissa close, gently kissing her hair and neck. He noticed the bracelet, and lifted Melissa's arm to examine it.

'It looks beautiful on you. Beauty on beauty.'

Melissa was smiling as she looked at him and he bent down kissing her softly first, and then more passionately.

'I've been thinking about doing that all week,' he said when their lips finally parted.

'Me too,' she replied. 'There are quite a few things

that I've been thinking about repeating,' she added mischievously.

'Well,' he said after a moment's pause, 'I think we should get a ring to match that bracelet. What do you think? Will you marry me?'

Before Melissa could respond she looked down as someone was tugging at her dress.

'Photo time,' Scott announced loudly, grabbing Melissa's hand and pulling her away from Andrew. In turn, Melissa grabbed Andrew's hand and they joined George and Helen under the pergola for a photo.

'OK, squeeze in,' the photographer demanded, 'that's looking better. Now it should look as though you're chatting. Say something.'

'Cheese,' Helen offered and they all laughed.

Melissa looked at Andrew and then at the photographer, and then called out boldly,

'I will.'

EPILOGUE

ogether they gently released the bottle into the Pacific Ocean. It was a way for them to say goodbye to their son together. They said nothing as they watched it float away with their messages of love. The sun was setting at the end of a beautiful day as they pulled up the anchor and sailed back to shore.

REFERENCES

Howard, Bart. 'Fly Me To The Moon', originally titled *In Other Words*, in album by of same name. Decca Music Group, April, 1954. Vinyl.

John, Elton. 'Something About the Way You Look Tonight'. *The Big Picture*. The Town House and Air Studios London. September, 1997. CD

Withers, Bill. 'Ain't No Sunshine When She's Gone'. *Just As I Am*, produced by Booker T. Jones. T .1971. Vinyl.

THANKS FOR READING

I hope you enjoyed reading *Over Byron Bay* as much as I did writing it. Great to learn what you thought if you have the time to pen me a few lines, and, if you feel so inspired, a review would be appreciated. You can email me at janeellyson@gmail.com and I'm also on twitter @janeellyson1- if you're a tweeter.

I've written a back story to the locations visited in Northern New South Wales and included a few photos from Bangalow, McLeod Shoot, Currumbin and of course, Byron Bay. They are all beautiful places and I would encourage you to visit them. You can obtain the back story by signing up for my newsletter at www. overbyronbay.com

I'm currently writing the sequel to *Over Byron Bay* called

Substitute Child. It is a thriller-romance set between Byron Bay and the Cote d'Azur. A deck hand in France discovers a bottle with a eulogy and letters inside. The bottle has floated all the way from Byron Bay in Australia to Nice. The discovery prompts a whirlwind journey for Charlotte Wyatt into the world of paparazzi, European royalty and the criminal underworld. If you are on my mailing list, you will receive advance notice of its publication.

Happy reading,

Best
Jane

www.overbyronbay.com
Twitter @janeellyson1

ABOUT JANE ELLYSON

Jane has a deep connection to the Far North Coast of New South Wales where *Over Byron Bay* is set. Her great grandparents owned a farm a little way out of Byron Bay and her grandparents were long term residents of Mullumbimby. She currently lives at Possum Creek, not far out of Bangalow – well she would if she was real - rather than being the pen name of someone who would prefer to remain anonymous. This is her debut novel.

NOTES

(1) NETS - The Newborn & pædiatric Emergency Transport Service

https://www.nets.org.au/

www.ingramcontent.com/pod-product-compliance
Lightning Source LLC
Chambersburg PA
CBHW030641110726
47901CB00002B/531